The Shark & other stories

Also by Leigh Swinbourne and published by Ginninderra Press
Away & other stories

Leigh Swinbourne

The Shark

& other stories

The Shark & other stories
ISBN 978 1 74027 674 0
Copyright © text Leigh Swinbourne 2011
Cover: Cathy McAuliffe Design

First published in this form 2011
Reprinted 2012
Reprinted 2016

GINNINDERRA PRESS
PO Box 3461 Port Adelaide 5015
www.ginninderrapress.com.au

Contents

One Winter's Afternoon 7
Face at the Window 13
The Willing Flesh 18
An Unexpected Meeting 54
Night Prey 58
The Shark 68

One Winter's Afternoon

Dr Leonard Fuller MB, BS, FRACGP huddles from the chill into his astrakhan overcoat, hands clenched in pockets, breath pluming before him like a spirit. Directly facing him is a faded weatherboard cottage, poor but squarely confident somehow, on a cracked concrete base surrounded by a bare yard pocked with rubbish and spare ashy tufts of grass. This is unexpected, the bareness, solitude. From a stock of working-class clichés he had imagined a cramped terrace, squeezed between like: squalling babies, talkback radio, sharp domestic squabbles in a foreign tongue, spicy kitchen smells… We always assume the proletariat more vital for some reason, Dickens and Dostoevsky probably the prime culprits. He, of all people, should have known better.

For it is very much a working-class suburb, but also an old industrial zone, so he has driven past untidy waste stretches and this property is adjacent to one of these, a half-built derelict estate. On the other side, fifty yards distant over a tangle of rusty barbed wire, a decrepit Gothic factory slumps silently, windows all eerily vacant like eye sockets. A factory like the one he worked in forty or so years ago when he'd known this suburb pretty well. Doesn't look like much has changed, now it all gradually comes back to mind. One of a sequence of endless lousy jobs, somewhere near, Taubman's Paints, scouring out recycled vats, dangerous industrial labour, stripped to the waist, poisonous air, hot as buggery. Supporting his older unmarried sister and her boy, and his pickled war-invalided father, all dead now, while powering through a medical degree five nights of the week. Where on earth had he found the energy, the drive? Belief and enthusiasm now seem relics as distant from him as these presently before him.

He digs the ferule of his umbrella into the footpath, uproots a dead weed. Not a cloud in the sky; why did he bring the bloody thing? He feels down, enervated, unusual for him, but probably simply because everything looks so drab and he had such a late night.

'You must come! Don't you care?'

The flatness of the place seems entirely at odds with the shrill urgency of the young female voice on the line that persuaded him out of the fug of his office. He hardly ever makes house calls now, particularly from the second surgery, and on such a raw day. But Pollock was tied up with the insufferable Mrs Macallister, the caller was insistent, and actually he has nothing much else to do.

The thought of his assistant makes him conscious of a slight foulness on the back of his tongue. Too much red wine (definition of an alcoholic: a man who drinks more than his doctor), though in this case a pretty justifiable over-indulgence in a vain attempt to ameliorate the dull convivialities of the previous evening. Dinner at the Pollocks was becoming almost a weekly event. He does not like Pollock, brash, opinionated, ambitious, and his perky arriviste wife. Of course, he himself had been much the same at that age, and this is perhaps why.

Other unpleasantries of the evening now crowd in on him. After he thought it was all finally over, drifting off on the electric blanket, his wife had turned to him, the most astonishing thing, they had not made love in well over a decade, and what with this and his over-consumption, he'd had to suppress a reflex to vomit. What on earth was she thinking? Had parvenu Pollock turned her on? Parvenu Pollock's priapic prick, bit of a medical legend from all accounts. That last girl, he had to let her go. Pity. To be honest, he wouldn't mind a shot himself at the young wife, enjoyed her bending to the oven when he went out to freshen his Scotch, imagined hiking her skirt. Fantasy all right, but in real life you had to endure the bloody conversation.

Not that he can endure any conversation these days. His wife at least respects this, days on end when they literally do not pass a word. What is conversation anyway when you break it down but exchange of information? And what information could they possibly have to exchange after all this time? Yet they had both been great talkers once, sitting up half the night, all that nonsense: politics, religion, literature, matters long since exhausted. These days he never even picks up a newspaper, let alone a novel. People saying the same things over and over to one another down the years. Why on earth do they do it? Sometimes he feels that it is only silence that makes life bearable. He could break with her of course, with them all for that matter, but even that seems far more effort than it is worth. Too much fuss; he has always hated fuss. Easier just to keep plodding on; line of least resistance.

Gingerly opening the gate on its single hinge, the picket fence is also half collapsed, a good kick would do for it, he picks his way fastidiously up uneven paving past yellow papers and crusty dog turds. The front door could also use a lick of paint. He raps the knocker firmly, importantly. The sound is swallowed, but definitely would have carried. Waits. Nothing. Raps again, louder. Nothing. A third time.

The breeze picks up, grit in his eyes and teeth. Must get that bridgework done; he's as bad as some of his patients in postponing the inevitable, old men always the worst. He couldn't possibly have made a mistake. He glances back at the gate: thirty-eight, same as his own house. He hears the woman's voice again, the exaggerated articulation, the hot edge of panic. Wrong street? Maybe there are two.

He crosses back over to the Mercedes, glossily conspicuous, tossing the umbrella onto the back seat where he has left the street directory. Street and directory correspond.

He returns to the front door and smashes the knocker repeatedly into its base, bangs the ball of his palm on the wood, shouts into the wind, making a spectacle of himself, if there were anyone around to see. He stops, and the sudden contrasting quiet spooks him. Maybe something serious has happened.

He makes his way around the house to the back, which appears weirdly as same as the front. An empty dusty yard, no back fence, the old night-soil lane exposed. A fly-screened back door bangs erratically in the wind, the inside door is latched back open. He enters.

The kitchen. Worn linoleum, dirty curtainless windows. He calls out again. No response. But everything seems orderly, plates and pots and pans neatly stacked on open unpainted wooden shelves. But it also looks dusty, unused. He handles a saucer, an old cheap willow pattern from his youth. There is no food about. The sink is dry, slightly stained, slightly foul. He turns the tap. A hollow sucking sound, but no water. He crosses to the fridge, again a design he remembers from the past, the modular-shaped top, once ludicrously thought to be modern, even futuristic. It is not running. He opens it, it is empty, the stale air carrying a faint but sharp tang of mould. On the bench there is a toaster, one of the ancient type that opens either side, and a pale green electric jug meshed with fine hairline cracks, black Bakelite lid, dry as the sink. Some equipment for living, but where is the life? Sunlight flowing from the windows seems to pin down the various objects as though they are permanent fixtures. He has a ridiculous intimation that the house is watching him, waiting to see what he will do. The hangover again.

He ventures up a carpeted corridor, fifties floral, maroon. Whoever designed these things? Musty. There are two bedrooms, one on either side and he pokes his head into both of them. The rooms are neat, again orderly, beds made with faded pink tufted-chenille covers, no clothes around, no bric-a-brac, presumably also unused.

Beyond the bedrooms, at the front of the house on either side, are the living room and master bedroom. From the living room he can see through sagging venetian blinds over to his car. Shabby lounge, a single ornament on the mantelpiece. Incredible! It looks to be an exact replica of a Dresden miniature he bought for his wife on their honeymoon in London thirty years ago, now long lost. Memory plays tricks, but still, it looks uncannily the same. He turns it in his hands, a young girl in peasant costume, pointed black shoes, bright blue dirndl, and the face, yes, unmistakable. He bought the figurine because the face was so much like his wife's. And she was once like this, slim, bright, laughing.

Another age. He had been so much in love; there had been nothing else. Impossible to believe.

He realises that for some reason while he has been holding the girl, examining her, he has also been holding his breath, and he now lets it out between his teeth with a long slow whistle. Upon which he finds he is on the verge of tears. Absurd.

He steadies himself and, model still in hand, enters the main bedroom. Here the air seems denser. Again, all is orderly and empty, except the covers of the bed are drawn back in what is comparatively wild disarray, and there is a large dark rust stain on the mattress sheet. He walks over and fingers it. Stiff. Old dried blood, although a strange discolouration at the edges makes it appear fresh, moist, where it blends into the cotton. He brings his fingers to his nose and for some bizarre reason smells his wife on them. A totally perverse olfactory illusion. Then from no motive he can credit, at that point or later, he places the figurine precisely in the centre of the stain. Suddenly the door knocker booms, scaring him half out of his wits. A surge of panic momentarily grips him. He races to the door and wrestles with the lock. How does the bloody thing work?

'Hang on!'

Finally it gives. The cold blows in. No one on the doorstep, or in the yard. Kids probably. He quickly looks over to the car. Nothing. Unless they are coming around the back.

He re-locks the door and retraces his steps down the hall and out the back door. No one. He returns to the front. Better give it away. A prankster? Or something else. Something sinister? Something, definitely, but what? He pauses. It is there right before him, but he just cannot get a grip on it. Silly nonsense, no doubt.

The westerly picks up, cutting through his coat. He walks back down the path and pauses again for a moment at the leaning gate, trying to think what, if anything, he should do. He waits, but nothing further happens and nothing comes to mind. If the call was genuine and the woman wants him, she'll ring again.

Now the sun has gone and the pale winter light is dimming in the open sky with a bleak, brief radiance. He looks across to where that light is focused, watches the broken shapes of abandoned buildings slowly blacken, coalesce, disappear, as the world itself slowly turns.

Queer business all right. The sealing kiss of the driver's door is comforting, final. Ignition, heater, radio. The car glides down the long street, takes the first corner and with a squeal of tyres accelerates away.

Face at the Window

Yesterday morning, rushing to work, I briefly saw the face of a young woman in a bus window, and that face has remained with me all of yesterday and all of today. I saw her while running, just after leaving my bus, I was a few minutes late, the bus always seems to run late these days, and I caught her looking directly at me through the pane. She was pretty, I guess she wouldn't have caught my eye otherwise, but it was not this that held me. It was the way she looked at me, not a look of desire, although I would like to think it had some desire in it, and not quite a look of longing, more of searching, perhaps hope, but also perhaps hopelessness. I felt somehow and for some reason that an important contact had been made even in a moment, and of course any possibilities from that contact cut off a moment later.

People in the street are naturally guarded, they use their eyes to block contact, but occasionally you catch them open, and you look straight into the depths. Lately I'm often unguarded. That girl and I, when we looked at each other, we were both like that, I'm sure, I'm not inventing it. If only I could see her again. No chance. I believe I might be in love with her.

I know this is ridiculous, but now I have reached that time of the afternoon when my mind wanders, there is a weight on my senses and spirit, a heavy blanket that half suffocates. It is hot, it is sometime after lunch and sometime before closing when there are not many customers, and the sun, as it leans towards the west, shines through the heavy tinted glass at the front and slowly, so slowly, creeps across the carpet to my desk. I know nothing more deadening than the creep of that mid-afternoon sun, and when it is actually on my desk, I cannot bear it any more and must get up and find something, anything, to do around the office.

My job is not a taxing one. I work as a clerk in a suburban business that is a franchise of a much larger business, in a relatively busy retail area, although one that is gradually decaying. Every second day it seems I see another vacant shopfront. My work is fairly boring, routine, but I do not mind too much. Well, I don't mind too much in the mornings when I am still fresh; nowadays I seem to mind in the afternoons. It is my fault, of course, that I do not have a more interesting and satisfying job. Some years back the business tried to offer me one. They moved me upstairs to train me, but I found the added responsibility and the politics and the pressure stressful, and I quickly saw that the new job would soon be as routine as the one I had left. So I asked to be put back. They took note of this, and I have not been asked to go anywhere else since. So I will work in this same job until I retire, which is unthinkable, unless I somehow find the energy to move.

My workmates are pleasant enough. I have no real problems with anyone here, although I don't seem to have much in common with any of them. I don't really understand why this is so. I don't understand why I am not interested in the same things that they are interested in, and don't even know what other, better, things I might be interested in.

There is a clerk who sits next to me who works exactly the same job, a fat neat boy named Tom. Tom's twin passions are collecting stamps and eating. It's funny to meet someone these days who still collects stamps, but he seems to get real pleasure from it, soaking the exotic little paper squares from the occasional overseas mail in a saucer of water on his desk. As for eating, he is a mindless glutton. Each lunchtime he consumes half a fried chicken and a large bucket of chips. He doesn't seem to enjoy his eating, he does it compulsively, automatically, while reading a tabloid. He is a heavy gambler too, on the TAB, but never wins.

Our supervisor is a nervy intense man named Barry. He has a prominent mole on one side of his face that if I were him I would have removed. Barry does not like Tom, although I can't see why, but since we do the same job, this is good for me. His passions – interests, I should call them – are girls, football and drink, particularly drink.

I just cannot believe how much my workmates drink. Every night they go to the pub, every night, and just sit and drink and say the same things to one another that they have been saying all day. It seems to me they must spend all of their money on alcohol, and I know they don't have much money. Some of them sometimes drink all night and come to work without any sleep, utterly useless. I don't know how they do it, or why they do it.

I join them every Friday night, I am obliged to if I don't want to become too much of an outsider. I can't say I enjoy it, although I don't really have anything better to do at home. I watch them all get drunk, and I get drunk with them because there is no choice and nothing else to do. Some become aggressive and want to fight, some become sexually excited; some, like me, just slump moronically. It is on these nights that I catch up on all the gossip of the week, who's sleeping with who, who's already spent all of their salary or is in trouble with their credit cards or the rent, who's had a letter of complaint written about them by a client or a customer. All the women get up and dance and all the men sit around and say obscene things about the women on the dance floor, particularly about the boss's secretary Rosanna, who is the most attractive and flirtatious girl in the office and who they all desire. Although I'm not attracted to her, I join in the jokes and comments and pretend I am. She has slept with some of the men but is after bigger game. I see her occasionally going out to lunch with smart real estate types, older men, probably married. I pass her in the street with them, laughing unnaturally at their jokes, and she doesn't acknowledge me. I don't mind.

At present in my area, my supervisor is having an affair with the new girl, Melinda. Barry is also married but he lives with his wife and kids three hours away by train. He took the job for a promotion. Occasionally, but increasingly, he does not make it home at nights.

Melinda takes too many days off sick and, I have heard, will soon be asked to resign.

I could describe these people some more to you, and the others in the office, but there is nothing much of interest to tell about any of them. I do not understand what they see in one another, why they are attracted to one another and why they want to make love, or why they get angry at one another and want to have fights. I am not judging them, please don't misunderstand me. If people wish to get drunk, fight and make love, that is surely their business. I just don't understand why they want to do it, that's all. I often think as I watch them move through their paces, doing what they always have done and always will do, and obviously finding meaning and interest along the way, that there must be something very wrong with me. Why aren't I attracted to the boss's secretary if every other male in the branch is? Why do I find football and drinking boring? And really, what do I have in my life that is better or more fulfilling than these activities? There is no reason for me to go home and leave them all, although I prefer to do so.

I live in a bedsit in a quiet suburban street nearby. There is nothing to do in my flat except watch the television, and I do this for a while when I get home, but after a few hours it begins to depress me and I turn it off. Recently I have been going out late at nights walking the streets, just walking up and down empty back streets for hours, just for something to do. I sometimes think I'm going mad.

Some years ago I did try and live the life of my fellow workers. I got drunk with them every night and even had an affair with a shy thin unattractive girl who showed an unexpected interest in me, a young girl straight out of school. She was not a virgin, unlike me, but she was a religious Catholic. The whole business was a disaster. I don't even want to think about it any more. She is on relieving staff and occasionally works at our office. We don't say a word to one another. My fellow workers wink at me and at one another, and are relieved that they don't have to think of me as a homosexual. I am too. This has been my only relationship, but I dream of girls; sometimes I dream of them all day until a vague type of longing seems to completely overwhelm me. I would like to meet a girl like me, but I have never met anyone like me, as far as I know. And what am I like after all?

Last week on the way to work, the bus passed a rainbow lorikeet that was fluttering, half crushed, in the middle of the road. The blood of the bird was mixed with its vivid green and orange and purple feathers, and as I watched it on the street there, struggling hopelessly, before the bus moved on, I felt an immense sadness, which I still have not managed to shake off.

Just an hour ago I looked up from my desk and thought I saw through the tinted glass the same girl who I'd seen through the window of the bus yesterday morning. To the amazement of my fellow workers, I suddenly rose up and raced into the public area, past the few customers, and out into the street, but I could not see her anywhere, although there were few people around. The bright glare hurt my eyes and wherever I looked up and down the street the hot afternoon sun reflected back a mocking glitter.

The Willing Flesh

For thirty of his fifty-six years, James Newman had lived in a small but comfortable flat in a gracious old tenement at Kings Cross. He did not like the neighbourhood, was fastidious by nature, and the filth left every morning by the varied mass that swept through Sydney's red-light area genuinely disgusted him. But the place was central and convenient, had a priceless harbour view, and had been inherited from a much-loved aunt via his mother, who drew satisfaction from him living there. Most of his customers lived in the eastern suburbs, particularly the well-heeled continental belt, and so were close at hand.

He lived alone, had never married, an only child of a young widow, from boyhood he had always known himself to be homosexual. But despite the proximity of the Oxford Street scene, promiscuity was foreign to him and for many a year he yearned for one true loving partner with whom he could live out his days, but this did not eventuate. By his late thirties he was more or less resigned to celibacy. This was not a big problem; he was shy and self-sufficient by nature and always found company stressful, even company he liked.

There was little to disturb his even, industrious days. He enjoyed his profession, a minor portraitist in oils. He had a talent; he knew its limitations. The modest income he steadily earned from a regular clientele was largely spent on delicacies and refinements, fine clothes, good food and wine, and particularly his great loves, the theatre and ballet.

One crisp autumn morning, James was meticulously placing the final dabs on the beloved only son of a Hungarian couple from Double Bay. He always took a special delight in painting children, their freshness and honesty, which faded so quickly. He was in unusually high spirits and the brushwork flowed easily. For the very first time he had received an official commendation for a work he had entered in the NSW Portraiture Prize, which he entered every year.

The portrait itself was straightforward enough, but the subject was somewhat unusual: Harold Holt, the prime minister who had tragically drowned, presumably alone, back in the mid-sixties in the treacherous currents off Cheviot Beach at Portsea. Because no body had ever been recovered, the incident still carried an aura of mystery and journalists periodically resurrected it. James had perused a magazine article on Holt which, for some reason he couldn't quite locate, particularly struck him, in fact inspired him. Not least, he supposed, because it revived in his mind a period of his own life that was memorable, his early adolescence, when he had developed his deep passion for the arts, which he now suspected was partly displaced sexuality. But the sights and sounds of the decade remained vividly in his mind, so out of nostalgia, or on a whim, and with a little time on his hands between commissions, he had painted Holt from a grainy print accompanying the article, and submitted the work without expectation. Every canvas he had ever painted, including all his previous entries to the prize, had always been on commission, so he was chuffed that his odd unique initiative in this instance had been rewarded.

He was taking a breather, dreamily admiring the eight-year-old subject who, as usual, he had slightly idealised, when the phone rang, startling him. For some inexplicable reason the answering machine had switched itself off. He carefully laid down his brushes, pressed the pause button on a newly purchased recording of Gluck's *Don Juan* ballet music, and lifted the receiver.

'I need to speak to Mr James Newman.' A mature female voice, imperious and resonant.

'Speaking.'

'Mr Newman, is it your Harold Holt at the Gallery?'

'Yes...'

'I require a portrait from you.'

'May I know to whom I have the pleasure of speaking?'

'Marjorie Turner. You don't know me.'

'Mrs Turner…'

'Miss.'

'I'm sorry. What kind of portrait were you interested in?'

'Are you engaged on any other projects at present?'

'Nothing urgent.'

'I'd like you to start working for me as soon as possible.'

'That should be all right. Now, the subject…'

'…is a little complicated, Mr Newman. Could you come and see me. I'm a paraplegic. I cannot leave the house easily.'

'Of course. Where do you live, Miss Turner?'

'Paddington. 36a Prince Street. Down below. You'll see the ramp. It's not difficult to find. Can you come today?'

'That's not possible, I'm afraid.'

'Tomorrow?'

'I suppose so. Yes of course, I mean.'

'Good. Eleven-thirty suit you?'

'Yes…'

'I'll see you then. Goodbye.'

The receiver beeped in his hand. He replaced it carefully in its cradle. How odd. She sounded a tyrannical dowager. Paddington. No doubt well off.

He returned to his canvas but now without success. His concentration had been broken. He persevered but it was useless. He took a break and then went back to it, but still could not pick up the thread. This had never happened to him before. What was the matter? For the present he would simply have to put the work aside.

Next morning it was cool and raining heavily. Intimations of winter. Such a nuisance to have to go out. James didn't own a car. He dug out his raincoat and umbrella and headed off. A train came readily and the place proved simpler to find than he had thought; in fact, by some serendipity he walked directly to it, a grand ornate three-storeyed Victorian terrace, immaculately restored. The whole street was a gem, actually, some of the finest architecture he had seen in this whole nineteenth- century district, fronted by tall and graceful eucalypts in a quiet winding dead-end. He might return when it was sunny and try a few sketches. 36a was, as the woman had said, 'down below', a flatette, presumably former servants' quarters, a small dark place hidden at the base of a short staircase behind a wrought iron railing and a row of potted geraniums. He noted the ramp.

No point standing in the rain. If he was too early for her he would find a coffee somewhere. He descended and rapped on the door.

'Come in, Mr Newman. It is unlocked,' boomed the voice from the phone.

James entered cautiously. Immediately he was struck by a smell of damp and felt heavy air in his lungs. Not so restored. The room was over-furnished in a drab 1940s style, the furniture and trappings were expensive and ugly, and in the centre of the room, dominating the place, bolstered with rugs and pillows in a large electronic wheelchair and tapping a cigarette into a tall stalk ashtray, was the most extraordinary-looking woman James thought he had ever seen in his life. The first and last thing you noticed about her was her head. It was enormous, square and brutal in shape. If she had not been a cripple, she would have been huge, very big-boned, thought James. Her wide jaw was set in a determined fashion in a jowly fleshy face. She had bright green eyes that looked like they never blinked and she wore a startling red wig, maybe the colour of her hair in her youth. Her face was plastered in pancake make-up, her cheeks rouged, her eyebrows stencilled and her lips glossy carmine. The general effect was as if for some peculiar reason she wished to appear as a coquette, which could not possibly have been the case.

But despite this facial grotesque affectation of youth, presumably ingenuous, James could see that she was in fact younger than he had assumed from her voice, probably about mid-fifties. She was clad in ornate black crepe and heavy jewellery: an amber necklace, a large silver brooch, bracelets and four or five chunky rings on her big bony hands.

'Come in, Mr Newman. I'm pleased to meet you.'

James approached and offered her his own delicate hand, but when she did not move a muscle in response, he withdrew his gesture and stood there awkwardly.

'Elspeth!'

A girl of about sixteen came running in. 'Yes, ma'am.'

'Do you drink tea or coffee, Mr Newman?'

'Black coffee, thank you.'

'I'll have the usual, Elspeth.'

The girl vanished.

'Have a seat, Mr Newman. You look as if I'm going to bite your head off.'

'Please forgive me, madam. I assure you I had no such notion in mind.' He placed himself gingerly on the edge of an armchair.

'Miserable day. Not that it really matters much to someone like me.' She fell into reverie.

There was a long silence, embarrassing only to James. The coffee and tea were served. He sipped at his cup. The dead quiet played on his nerves; he couldn't even hear the rain.

He spoke, and the sound of his own voice startled him: 'You were saying that you admired my portrait in the competition.'

She suddenly turned and looked at him with her enormous head and green eyes. Searchlights on a turret. 'I think to be a painter must be the most wonderful thing in the world. I have always thought that, but I felt it most strongly when I saw your painting. Even a composer or a writer cannot experience their work at a single instant, cannot say, There, this is what I have done.'

Enthusiastic flattery was the last thing James had expected. He started to relax. 'But consider, my dear Miss Turner, neither do they have to part with their creation. They always have access to it. I thank you for your kind thoughts, but I am no genius and what little glamour there is to my work I'm afraid I have long lost the sense of. I will grant you it is an admirable way to make a living, and I am grateful to be able to do so, but ultimately I paint for the money, and when I have made sufficient, I will retire.'

She looked away again, chewing this over. 'I cannot believe that.'

'Nevertheless, it is true.'

'May I detain you with some notions of mine, Mr Newman? It is so rarely I get to talk to an artist.'

James reminded himself she was a paying customer. 'Of course.'

She tilted her head back and focused somewhere above and behind him, as though addressing a third party. 'I have always believed,' she said, 'in the presence of, how shall I put it, an invisible world, a perfect world of archetypes of which our world is one degenerate distorted version. We move in corruption, Mr Newman, because we lack vision. This is our fall. We cannot penetrate beyond our gross senses. I have always seen the artist as a kind of agent, or perhaps a channel, someone able to tap into this invisible world.'

'Very Platonic,' James mused. 'I am not such a romantic, and I am vain enough to grant my intellect a more active part in the whole process. And also, perhaps if you painted, forgive me, you might have more respect for a thorough technique. A good deal of spontaneity can be taught in the arts, you know.'

'But technique is only ever your key, Mr Newman.'

'I don't see it quite that way.'

'You must admit the existence of aesthetic ideals.'

James sighed inwardly. This was becoming tiresome. 'Many painters don't. In fact, the fashion nowadays is more to regard any critical apparatus as wholly pertaining to a certain time, place and people. Now, I don't say I go along with this. I believe man to be much the same the world over and I do believe in certain aesthetic absolutes, as I do in certain moral absolutes, I suppose, but this is still a far cry from your invisible world.'

'Yet it is there!' She eyeballed him fiercely. 'I have known it! I have seen it!'

James was taken aback. He tried to shrug casually. 'I do not say I disbelieve you, my dear lady, but still, it is not my experience.'

'I don't believe that, Mr Newman. When I saw your picture of Holt, an extraordinary man by all accounts…'

'An unexceptional prime minister.'

'But an extraordinary lover, you know.'

This stunned James, shocked him even.

She continued, 'When I saw your portrait, I felt, I knew that you had tapped something vital. Something came through the middle-aged lines of that face, Mr Newman. Do you know what it was? It was one of the archetypes of human beauty.' Her eyes shone.

James shifted uncomfortably.

'I have another notion for you, Mr Newman.'

James was wishing he had not come.

'The more a painting is reproduced, the more power it possesses.'

'You mean the more it appears in prints and coffee-table books and the like?'

'Precisely.'

'But surely you must allow that if the *Mona Lisa* had been seen by no one except Da Vinci, and then lost, it still would have been a great painting.'

'I do not allow it, sir, for what is potential if it is not manifested?'

James thought of her dead limbs. She could not help but be bitter.

'Holt would not have been a man of power and attraction unless he acted in the world. Once the artist has finished his painting, it is his no longer. It takes a life of its own, a career of influence and fascination.'

'That is interesting. I confess it has never occurred to me before. But forgive me, I have a sitting later this afternoon,' he lied.

'I forget myself. You must be a businessman, Mr Newman.'

'Unfortunately so. Now, did you wish for a portrait of yourself?'

'Me?' She burst out. 'Incredible! Of course not!'

'A relative, or a friend?'

James saw the strident articulate confidence start to evaporate. She shrank into herself slightly. 'No. This portrait, you need to understand, Mr Newman, is rather of a delicate and personal nature.'

'You can rely on my discretion.'

'That's not what I mean. It's just that it's difficult for me to say it.'

'Please take your time.'

'Well, what I wanted to ask of you was, you may have surmised that I have never been married. To be frank with you, Mr Newman, I doubt whether I ever could have been capable of sex anyway, such as it is depicted in popular fiction at least. I have been in my present state of incapacity since childhood. I have no sensation below the chest.'

James felt extremely embarrassed, but out of respect for the sincerity and difficulty of her confession, struggled successfully not to show it. He wished again that he had never come to this incredible interview.

'Yet,' she continued, 'I am, perhaps unfortunately, a passionate person. You are an artist. I trust you understand what I mean. I have desired and do desire a mate, as do most of us. You see, when I saw your painting of Holt, I tried to suppress the idea you understand, and yet it kept returning, and so why I have asked you here, you must consider what I am saying carefully, I do not make jokes, Mr Newman. What I was going to ask you is, whether you would consider the possibility of undertaking a commission, to paint for me a lover.'

'I'm sorry?'

'Yes, a lover.' The confidence returned. 'I am aware that this is an unusual request, and yet it must be done, and you are the man to do it.'

James sat flummoxed.

'I am an individual of no small means.'

'But Miss Turner, what you are saying is so fantastic, so nebulous. Paint you a lover? What do you mean by that? I am a painter, that is all, nothing more. I cannot create things in that sense. And anyway, I cannot get inside you and see through your eyes. It is not a matter of money. Don't you see, I must fail.'

'I don't see that, and anyway since I am paying it is my problem. I'm willing to take the chance that you will not fail, and pay you handsomely into the bargain whatever happens. Do you accept my offer, sir, my challenge?'

'But how can such a thing be effected? Always I work from a model, photographs, something...'

'And so you will this time. I know him. I will describe him to you. Do you accept my commission, Mr Newman?'

James thought it over. He was intending to say no, but when he opened his mouth, to his own surprise he answered, 'Why not? No offence intended. I honestly think it is a doomed idea, but if you insist, I will try. But I have no faith at all that I will please you.'

'Let me worry about that.' Her voice had a touch of impatience, even anger. 'Now, you said you had another sitting.'

'Yes.'

'I will delay you no longer. I want the portrait painted here. We will start next week at this time, if that is suitable. Can you bring your equipment?'

'Well, to begin with I will only use a notebook, until you are entirely satisfied, and I have something concrete to work on.'

'Good. Remember what I have said. I look upon paintings as the primitives looked upon their works of art. With our veneer of sophistication, we have lost the fundamental idea of what these things really are, objects of power, real spiritual power and influence. Well, until next week then, Mr Newman.'

And James found himself out on the street, with all ordinary suburban things around, wondering vaguely where he had been and what had happened. It was still raining heavily. He had forgotten that. A taxi cruised past and he hailed it. Through the back window he watched the shiny wet streets float past as if in a dream.

By the time he was home, he had decided definitely not to accept the commission. It was absurd. He paced his flat nervously trying to summon up courage and the right words with which to confront the formidable Miss Turner. He paced until his nerves were in a complete jangle. This would never do.

He pulled a chair over to the window, lit a cigarette and poured a dry sherry. The tobacco and alcohol soothed. He watched the grey rain falling into the harbour. The incessant whisper calmed him further. Why not accept? Bizarre, certainly, and, as he had said, he would probably be unsuccessful in what he had to offer, but no one would be any the wiser, and then there was the money. There was no doubt the old duck was loaded. A background of wealth and indulgence; one did not want to know the details. So why not string along for a while, humour her, and see what came of it.

But there was more. As he sat there listening and watching the rain, the whole project began to take on a peculiar fascination for him. She wanted a lover, he chuckled inwardly, pity mixed with distaste. How frail we all were, really. The self-absorption of a child combined with the desires of a woman, and a confined woman. All that contained energy, and passion, as she had said.

Who would be her ideal man, if man it was? No, it would be a man. Maybe he should make it one of his own past lovers. A practical joke, a jape. No, he was a gentleman. He would honestly try and realise her vision – that is, if she had any clear idea of what she wanted herself. An absurd notion, but rather an interesting one when you considered it. He had never actually created from pure imagination before, wasn't quite sure what that meant. He would lean on her, make her be specific. She wanted him to paint her lover? She thought he was the agent, the channel? Fine, she would have to produce the goods. He was a skilful painter. He knew it. If he failed in such a ridiculous enterprise, the fault was hers, surely.

He tried to put the project from his mind for the remainder of the day but somehow it persisted. Nevertheless, he finished his work for the Hungarians, and then, since nothing else was pending, decided to make preliminary preparations for the 'unknown' portrait.

His stretchers were all pine, too cheap for a job like this. This was unique and it demanded the best. So off to the city and his regular art shop for a frame of the finest hardwood. Now the project began to feel like some fantastic game. He started to enjoy himself. What size, he thought, as the train rattled merrily along to Town Hall. A large portrait, imposing, surely. Then the canvas. What tooth to choose? Must be fine. He was half imagining a portrait of a Renaissance villain, the type of character Browning would have characterised. And he would fill this vaporous conceit, which it seemed he must paint, with the most explicit detail. Yes, nothing but the finest linen.

He returned home with his trophies. He had a ticket for the theatre that night: Molière at The Wharf. He had just enough time to stretch and staple the canvas and grab a bite to eat before leaving for the show. He worked carefully, moving slowly around with the staple gun, correcting any slack in the corners. Finally he was satisfied. He pressed it lightly in the centre, just enough give, not too tight. He loved the feel of a new canvas. Then he cooked up some pasta, put on a tie and coat, and headed back to the city.

James sat happily in the snug dark of the auditorium while seventeenth-century French high society displayed its complex self-consciously amusing agonies. The play was brilliant, the performance fine, he was well entertained, and yet not completely engaged. A theatre critic in his position would say something to the effect that the performance 'had everything' but 'lacked a certain essence', 'an indefinable vitality', 'had missed the true spirit', something in that line. James was more honest and less vain. He knew that tonight the problem lay in himself. A strange restlessness had possessed him. Increasingly, he saw imposed on the bright action of the play the white expanse of the canvas sitting solitary in his dark apartment.

At interval, he took a Chablis outside onto the balcony and stared not up at the brilliant lights of the Bridge, but down at the inky water and again saw the white ghost of his canvas, floating indefinitely in the cool insubstantial medium.

Again in the second half he could see the frame, more clearly now.

He forgot the play and thought only of the portrait. No distinct image came into his mind, but there was a presence, undeniably. He could sense it, but not quite see it. He felt so strange. Perhaps he was coming down with something.

He wandered out of the theatre before the play had finished, a thing he had never done before in his life. His footsteps sounded eerie echoing off the long wooden boards down the empty hallway, as though he was being followed, as though he were following himself.

He walked out into a blustery night. A cliff wall of The Rocks stretched up above him. A strange dappling of light briefly flitted across its rough uneven surface, then darkness reclaimed it. He felt he was lost in a deep canyon. He continued unthinkingly. Suddenly he stumbled over a soft shape. He received a fright but kept his balance. It was the inert body of a large dog. Nowhere near the road, it seemed to have fallen off the top of the cliff, an odd accident for an animal. He looked up to the old iron railings a hundred feet or so above him, then back down to the corpse. It had not been dead long, the limbs were still loose, and most extraordinary of all, whether it was a trick of the night or just the peculiar features of this brute, its face seemed to be contorted into an aspect of inexpressible horror, an aspect almost human. James shook himself and walked on.

Up the empty streets, past The Hero of Waterloo, an island of riotous noise in the larger silence, and down through the Argyle Cut. The black mossy sandstone walls sweated with damp. Here, notoriously, had fought the razor gangs of the dreaded Push, vicious men cruelly slashing one another for pride and pleasure. Shaking off their ghosts, he strolled further on down to the harbour front where everything was bright and alive: jugglers and buskers, lovers and families. How pathetic they all seemed, all their trivial fun and jollity. Why? What had got into him tonight?

He caught a train home, smiling inwardly at himself, but when he opened the door of his flat and saw the canvas stationary in the dark, waiting, the strange mood returned. He switched on the light. What was wrong? Nothing. He poured a sizeable cognac and sat down comfortably with a favourite recording, a Schubert quartet, till again he felt relaxed and content and thought he could sleep. He prepared for bed but, on a whim, before switching off the light, he turned the canvas around to face the wall.

Next morning, with bright sun streaming in, he felt ashamed at his fancies of the previous evening. He mixed the glue for the canvas: two-thirds warm water, one-third Aquadhere; he found that the traditional rabbit skin glue tended to attract mould in the humid Sydney air. The three coats of this on the canvas was the only work he was able to do the whole day. He couldn't seem to fix his mind on anything mildly productive, so mid-afternoon he abandoned himself to deliberate holiday, taking a lengthy stroll through Centennial Park.

But the unsettling moods persisted throughout the week. He could do nothing, save put down the three coats of oil primer, with sanding, in preparation for the Turner portrait. The oddness and forthcoming problems associated with this one work seemed to blot everything else from his mind, and his mind was so restless. He had not known anything like it since adolescence. He seemed as the weather, shifting, undecided, as it was fitfully, inevitably, turning towards winter. He continued his walks through the park, wandering in the long damp grasses past lonely forests of paperbark while, high above, heavy-bellied clouds hung uncertainly in a sky darkening the opaque colours of the lakes. How strange everything seemed, everything normal. Something was happening to him. He had come to some turning point in his life, but what it was, and what it meant, he could not see.

Finally Tuesday came around, and when he woke that morning after uneasy sleep, he realised how much unconsciously he had been waiting for the day. The minutes seemed to tick away to the appointed time, and then he was almost late; he had misplaced his sketchbook.

Feverishly he ran down the long escalator and just jumped a train. He had to walk briskly to reach the house on time. He paused outside for a few moments to compose himself, then descended and knocked confidently.

'Come in, Mr Newman.'

The spider was in her lair just as he had left her. He thought he might have exaggerated her in his imagination but, on the contrary, the sight of her shocked him anew, that massive head and red wig, those piercing green eyes shining with vitality. She had waited for this day too, when he would be an instrument of her will and fantasy. On her ground, caught in her strong circle of influence. He saw now how successfully Marjorie Turner had made her disability her strength. She was focused, drew attention, compelled others to attend to her needs through her necessity and her money. She need only command, and the tone of her commands showed that she had done this all her life.

He sat with his notebook and pencil wondering what would happen next. Slowly, without any preamble, as if in a trance, she began to describe the portrait in her mind. James listened carefully. She seemed to have a very precise idea of what she wanted. Extraordinary, really. She had obviously imagined this man right down to the last detail. It reminded him of his own youthful fantasies. Just as well they were only dealing with the head!

As she talked on, her big body became tense and her face animated with desire, almost as if an earlier or different version of her was trying to break through. Here was the formidable Miss Turner displaying herself before James nakedly, even with abandon, and yet she seemed not at all vulnerable. Her desire needed no excuse or explanation; it was hers and therefore fully justified itself. She was not concerned what others thought; they only existed to serve her needs.

James sketched, hardly knowing what he was meant to be doing, and yet he sketched fluently, and presumably by her occasional commendations, accurately. So complete was the picture in her mind that it seemed to hold an almost hallucinatory quality for her. At each turn, James despaired of nearing her vision, but at each turn she egged him on with exclamations at his growing success. It was uncanny. Never, it seemed to him, had he drawn with such facility, and particularly of a subject of which he had no prior knowledge. It was as though his hand were being guided.

After six completed sketches, a definite face and character had emerged, and James seriously felt he had sufficient material with which to start painting. He looked at his work and was amazed, and then at his watch. The time had simply flown; he had entirely forgotten about lunch. Miss Turner, seemingly even more formidable in her happiness, was obviously fully confident of the eventual success of the whole mad venture. James took some careful notes from her concerning colouring, then gathered up his materials and bid the strange lady farewell until the same time next week.

Again he found himself standing on the footpath outside her home stunned. However, this time it was because he was…exhausted. Yes, that was it. Drained. Perhaps he wasn't well after all. All those damp walks in the autumn weather might have given him a chill. He wandered around the corner and up the street until he found a café. He ordered coffee and quiche. He felt so tired, but couldn't seem to relax. Presumably he had overstrained himself. He didn't feel hungry but ate the food anyway. Then he sipped his coffee slowly and lit a cigarette.

As he sat there, trying to relax, the sketches returned forcibly to his mind. He saw each progression so clearly, it seemed like polishing a mirror, or cleaning successive layers of grime off an old master. Well, better to let them work through his system rather than try and block them. In his mind he considered their sequential evolution, their coerced direction, alone in the empty corner of the café with the nicotine smoke curling around him.

Suddenly he saw his portrait in full vivid colour. This gave him such a fright that he seized up, knocking his cup noisily. The waitress looked across. This had never happened to him before. He had never suffered inspiration like this, had never fully believed in it, in Blake and Coleridge and the others, had half thought them all charlatans, in reality careful plodders like himself, only much better. But here it was, right before him. Who was this man who stared at him so arrogantly, appropriating this empty space? Where had he come from? He must paint him. He had to paint him now!

James paid his bill and raced out the door. He hailed a cab and sat nervously in the front seat, willing the driver to speed. He bolted up the stairs of his apartment. Before him the canvas, a shining vacancy, waiting.

He lightly touched the sizing, feeling it as though it were a living surface, shivering slightly as he did so. He began to mix his paints. First he put in the coloured ground, a raw sienna, then, using a mixture of pure gum turpentine with thin oil paint, he roughly washed in the dark tones of the composition, the shadows. So, quickly, he had a rough overall sketch of the head in Van Dyke brown.

Then a peculiar thing happened. He paused to look at his half creation and suddenly, momentarily, he felt that the canvas had a depth and he could see the head quite clearly, except that he was looking at it through some kind of dark veil, like a hologram. He had a weird sensation that while painting, instead of laying surfaces on, he was actually stripping them away, the same idea as in the café.

Again he worked feverishly, forgetting all time and place, starting to fill in the basic volumes with colour, sharpening the three-dimensional effect. First he used earthy colours, pink ochres and flesh tones, employing thin oily washes allowing the underpainting to show through. He kept layering washes and lightening up the portrait. Then, gradually, he used colours more opaque, less transparent, adding odd touches of white.

Finally, with his fine detail brushes he produced the graded complexities of tone and form. Last of all, as was customary, James painted the eyes. He had been resisting the eyes. He had felt an urge to paint them first, but had held back, allowing habit to support an ungrounded apprehension of giving his creation the spark of life. But now he knew he was ready; more, was driven to do it. He dabbed in the tiny white gleam in each pupil, then stood back to regard the finished product.

Night had long fallen. James had been painting for about eight hours. He had not left the easel. But there was light in the room. The moon was full in a clear cold autumn sky, and he had hardly noticed he had lost the day. He switched on the overhead fluorescent tube, rubbed his tired eyes, and realised that his arm and neck were strained, his bladder was bursting and he was starving.

But the portrait. He first noticed that the background of the picture was much darker than he had originally intended. Jutting out from this with bright shocking clarity was the face James had seen so sharply in the café, Miss Turner's 'lover'. It was a spotlight effect; the features were almost overdone, and yet they were incredibly lifelike, at once lifelike and larger than life: the full sensual face, the thick lips, the hooded determined stare of the eyes. The character of the face, the essential quality of the man, that most subtle and difficult thing, James had somehow rendered with disarming ease. It was a single flashing instant in a life, yet captured in such a way that suggested an entire existence, perhaps an entire world. He stepped back, took it in, took him in. Yes, it was the total man, and James was amazed to see what *he* had done, and still might do.

Strong and virile, in early middle age, aggressive, forceful and suavely attractive. He was on a three-quarter angle, as though he had been looking the other way and James had just caught his attention, just caught his eye. He looked as if he resented this interruption, would resent any interruption, and yet he also looked as if he wished to come from the dark and seize that busy outside world he himself had just noticed. He wore a plain white Renaissance smock and his greasy black hair hung down in unruly curls to his shoulders. His eyes were a beautiful and unique lapis colour; James wasn't sure how he'd created this tone. Yet they were sinister, and fully focused on the viewer.

Holbein, Titian, Bronzino, Rembrandt; James had travelled to Europe many times and gazed with wonder at the great classical portraitists, asking why he was in the game, why anyone was. But after everything, maybe this was why. Never had he done anything remotely approaching this anonymous unpremeditated work. Although he would never have told a soul, he had considered all his portraits to be a compromise of greater or lesser degree. He could capture likeness accurately, but little more. But not this. How had he done it? And so unselfconsciously. He looked at it and looked at it and slowly a rare joy stole over him. It was incredible, extraordinary, but there it was physically and undeniably before him. With this single achievement, James hitherto quotidian life suddenly blazed with substantial meaning. Here, these last few hours, somehow, he believed he had truly created something deathless.

But now he saw there was another matter. Normally with any portrait, the painter brought something of themselves to the work. Even with the most honest and ruthless of artists, a portrait was always, to some extent, an interpretation. But here, and James had never seen this before, there was no interpretation. There was nothing of him in this; the subject dominated wholly.

The paint was still wet. He would not touch it again. He could not. A rational panic seized him that he had not painted with his usual caution, had not allowed the various surfaces to dry properly. Perhaps the paint would shortly break up, and yet it all looked so accomplished, so finished. He would wait and see, but the thing seemed to him beyond ordinary physical laws.

It was too intense. He could bear it no longer. He turned the canvas to the wall as he had done on the night he was beset by phantoms. With the face out of sight, James experienced enormous release as though out of the grip of a spell. He was utterly spent. He sat on the couch and wept. After a while, he pulled himself together. He should get some food. He could not eat here, in the same room. It was impossible. He grabbed a jacket and walked out into the night.

A cold gritty wind blew up Macleay Street. James walked into it towards the hub of the Cross. Everything seemed unreal: the light vicious crowd, the spruikers, the neon-garish dens, the hookers, the homeless, the druggies, the tourists. None of these endlessly passing empty-eyed faces were living, had ever known what life meant, what it could hold. Life was in his flat facing a blank wall, more vivid, with more purpose and object. The lover had known life because he wanted and valued life, whereas these people did not. They took this precious gift with levity, and with equal levity some of them lost it.

Re-entering his flat, James was struck by the sharp smell of turpentine and linseed oil as though by a distinct presence, like an artistic body odour. Despite his exhaustion, he felt he would never be able to sleep with this, but that night he slept soundly for the first time since the day of the initial telephone call. And he woke feeling a miracle had occurred. He immediately went to the portrait to confirm this. Then he rang Miss Turner.

The maid answered and brought her to the phone.

'Mr Newman?'

'I trust I'm not disturbing you, Miss Turner.'

'You have finished the picture.'

'Yes.' James was nonplussed.

'Are you happy with it?'

'I think it's the finest thing I have ever done.'

'Better than the Holt portrait?'

'Much.'

'I am very eager to see it.'

'It's not quite dry but I can bring it around tomorrow.'

'Good.'

'Same time?'

'Till tomorrow, Mr Newman.'

Marjorie Turner was ecstatic. A little of the romantic that, James thought, surely must underlie such a peculiar commission, again seemed to break through her hard-boiled exterior. She was not a woman used to giving praise and was loud and pompous about it. She inadvertently insulted James by articulating his own incredulity at his accomplishment, then handed him a cheque well above the agreed price, told him she would choose a different frame, and more or less dismissed him. For now that he had delivered this painting, provided what she had wanted, he became superfluous. He saw that all the time he had really been like poor harried Elspeth, just another servant.

Weeks passed, and James applied himself to new works, but could not seem to settle comfortably into his former rhythm. Certain words with Miss Turner continually returned to haunt him. The painting, perhaps his sole effort of such quality, was out of his hands and in those of an eccentric and lonely woman, in fact her exclusive property. He had never before fussed about loss of ownership of a piece, content to regard any commission as belonging to the client, even prior to painting. But so much of him had gone into this, such energy and commitment, and something else less definable. It was as though the painting had taken a living part of him. And there was a further matter too, also increasingly needling him: his reputation.

James had never been particularly ambitious, largely because he had never regarded himself as an outstanding talent. But with this work he knew he had entered, if only fleetingly, that empyrean of select individuals who made art that actually mattered, art that people wrote and talked about and that influenced other artists, made people gasp as he had gasped at his first consideration of the completed canvas, as though someone else, far more gifted, had painted it. He wanted the Sydney arts world, and also the wider world, to know of this painting.

So when James's gallery offered to include some of his work in an upcoming group exhibition, he immediately thought of Miss Turner. He had not spoken to her since delivering the portrait, and when he rang he was reminded why.

'Miss Turner?'

'Mr Newman. What do you want?'

'How are you keeping?'

'Well enough.'

'Are you still happy with the portrait?'

'Of course. Why have you disturbed me, sir?'

'I was wondering whether it would be possible for you to loan the painting, for a short time, for an exhibition my gallery is mounting.'

'Out of the question.'

'It is not damaged?' A fear clutched James.

'It is as you remember it, Mr Newman, better, now that it is properly mounted. It is magnificent. He is magnificent.'

'I assure you every care will be taken, and insurance and all that type of thing.'

'You seem to forget that I have a special relationship with this work.'

Even on the phone, James blushed. 'I would be entirely discreet as regards that, Miss Turner.'

'I don't doubt it, but it's not the point.'

'I'm sorry?'

'I don't think we need continue this conversation.'

'Miss Turner, I will wear my heart on my sleeve. Your portrait is the finest thing, by far, I have ever done.'

'I know.'

'I doubt whether I will ever do anything as fine again.'

'You won't.'

'You must see how important it is to me that this painting is displayed to the public and critics, even if only for a short time. I repeat, every care will be taken.'

'Sir, I don't give two hoots for your reputation. I have learnt not to ask too much from life, because I haven't been given much to begin with. What little I want, I now believe I have, and I have paid good money for it. Goodbye, Mr Newman.'

'Madam, I implore you…'

She cut him off.

James plunged into depression. How could he possibly get the thing away from the harpy? At this rate it would never see the light of day. And who knows what might happen to it? Who was she anyway, this Miss Turner? A bitter and deprived solitary who did as she pleased and was unable to distinguish fantasy from reality. A lover, she wanted! What perverse desires had she conjured in the watches of the night? He had never really understood women, their suffocating needs. A reflexive misogyny, born from fear, embarrassment and misunderstanding began to surface in his mind. How could he handle her? Bring her round?

Perhaps he could persuade her through official channels. His gallery owner, Peter Le Fevre, was one of the most respected and influential figures in Sydney art circles and briefly, long ago, a lover of James. The legend of his charm was legion and, James ruefully considered, well founded. In his time, Peter had wheedled patronage out of all types – macho businessmen, soulless politicians, philistine society dames, air-headed celebrities – all difficult and vain in their different ways. If Peter couldn't tickle the old spider, nobody could.

James leant on him to write her a long prosy letter and, after a time, she replied, agreeing to release the portrait for the period of the exhibition only. James was beside himself. Whether Peter had hit just the right tone, or whether Miss Turner had had some strange change of heart he didn't know. It didn't matter. His masterpiece was to be seen.

As opening night approached, James grew increasingly apprehensive, even more rattled than he remembered being prior to his very first exhibition. He had not seen the painting since originally handing it over. Maybe it was not as good as he thought; he'd been caught out like this a few times in the past. Maybe his odd mental state at the time prompted (he assumed) by the peculiar nature of the commission had led him to make an over-estimation, even a false judgement, which the sentimentality of memory had further compounded.

On the other hand, when he thought clearly and steadily about the work, when he brought its vivid entity to mind, he always returned to his original conviction that it was the best thing by far he had ever done. And he supposed, even allowing for some exaggeration, given his established reputation and success, given his proven skills, that that made it a pretty damn good painting. He was right to invest hope in it, surely.

So his confidence waxed, waned and waxed again until finally, heart in mouth, he stood beside his old flame Peter Le Fevre before a large plain parcelled rectangle in the hushed privacy of the closed gallery.

'Now, let us see what all the fuss was about, James, my dear,' said Peter, a slim dapper queen, overstated and flamboyantly Australian in a way that James emphatically was not.

James removed the wrapping, unbuckled the casing, and positioned the painting on an easel against a neutral blank wall. Then both stood back to regard it in the clear mid-morning light. James tensed. It exceeded his memory. But was his judgement correct? Yes, surely Peter must see.

Peter was standing stock still, his mouth a little agape. 'Why darling, how did you ever come to do such a thing? What on earth possessed you?'

'I really believe it to be my best piece,' James responded with genuine humility.

'It's a fucking masterpiece, you silly old dag. I just cannot believe it. Who the hell is he?'

'I don't know.'

'What do you mean, you don't know?'

'Basically, I painted it from my imagination.'

'Go and pull the other one, will you?'

'Seriously.'

'You're protecting that old cow in some way, aren't you.'

'I'm telling you the truth, Peter. You can believe me or not, as you wish.'

'Now don't get your knickers in a knot, James. I'm just a little amazed, that's all. In fact, more than a little amazed.' Peter slowly paced the empty gallery, viewing the work from varying perspectives.

'She wanted a portrait. She didn't know of whom, or care. Just something to hang on the wall, that's all. She'd seen my Holt picture. So I just cooked the whole thing up, so to speak.'

'Cooked the whole thing up? Bit of a doll, isn't he? James, level with me, did you paint this bloody thing or not, because if you're trying to make a monkey out of me after all these years, you'll come a cropper, darling, fair dinkum.'

'You know my work. Does it look like me, my technique?'

'Your technique, yes, definitely, nothing else. It's fucking incredible, you know. It's like a bloody Bellini or something. What can I say? The more I look at it, the more I'm absolutely gobsmacked.'

'I felt that it was very special when I finished it.'

'You were right, James. And I will not be the last to say it.'

He wasn't. The portrait was at once acclaimed. Article upon article appeared in the press, night after night the gallery was packed, a constant throng buzzing around James's canvas. His reputation soared. Lucrative commissions appeared out of nowhere, potential work to last him comfortably for years.

Then, on the back of all that, a retrospective exhibition of his entire *oeuvre* was hastily cobbled together by the NSW Art Gallery, a great public honour, and although this generally disappointed, in that none of his other work came up to the mark of the portrait seen at the Le Fevre Gallery, the quality of this single, once-exhibited picture was sufficient to launch and sustain James as an artistic celebrity.

By this time, Miss Turner had jealously resumed her property, and was not taking any calls. But the fuss seemed to go on regardless. The work was reproduced in every new book on Australian art and James started to see the bloody thing staring out at him from poster shops, cafés and restaurants, domestic dining rooms and even the occasional petrol station (he had bought a car by now).

For not only was the painting a masterpiece, it was a popular masterpiece. Like Da Vinci's *Mona Lisa* or Michelangelo's *David*, its greatness seemed to reach out to all. All were compelled by the unreal magnetic fascination of this man, *Il Cacciatore*, The Hunter, as Peter titled him and as he generally came to be known for his bold and sinister appearance.

James had, out of the blue, attained the apotheosis of his career. Over time, he came to accept it as a never to be repeated accomplishment, a one-off. So resignedly but not unhappily, he settled back to enjoy the laurels of a single outstanding effort, admitting privately to himself that it was more than he thought he would ever achieve anyway, more than artists of his calibre usually achieve.

Two years passed, and James was still being hounded over the painting, by the painting. Its non-visibility seemed only to further stimulate interest and discussion, as though *Il Cacciatore* was a famously reclusive actor or author rather than an anonymous two-dimensional image. Peter, as James's agent, had potential buyers, private collectors and public galleries offering large sums but Miss Turner was not biting. James, of course, was keen to wrest it from her too, but only once did he manage to get through to her:

'I only let it out to stop you all bothering me, Mr Newman. Obviously I miscalculated.'

Another year passed with no let-up. Now international art circles began to show interest. There was to be an extensive retrospective of twentieth century Australian art at the Museum of Modern Art in New York. The curators requested *Il Cacciatore* for the exhibition.

Again James contacted Miss Turner to try and explain the situation. 'It's a matter of international prestige. It's important for Australian art as a whole.'

James had actually managed to wangle his way back into the basement flat, the Turner 'burrow', as he thought of it. *Il Cacciatore*, against the far wall, dominated the main room, was the room. How vigorous and menacing it looked! How alive!

Miss Turner had changed subtly, James thought. She was less caustic, less waspish, even passive in a way, her eyes somehow full of both a strange satisfaction and an expectancy. But of what?

'Do you really think, Mr Newman, serious international attention will be focused on my portrait?'

'Absolutely.'

'And so might it become famous beyond these shores?'

'I am sure of it. It is happening already.'

'I was never going to let it out again, you know. I am too possessive, but I have since been persuaded that I must. With such acclaim it will increase in power.'

'Yes, I remember your idea. Well, if you believe that and want it' (but who could possibly have persuaded her?) 'here is your opportunity.'

'But only…'

'What, my dear lady?'

She leaned forward and spoke sotto voce. 'No one must ever know of the genesis of this work. Swear to me, Mr Newman.'

'I have never breathed a word to anyone and I will continue to preserve your privacy. Depend on it.'

'It is more than just me. We cannot ever tell our secret, you and me, and Elspeth too. Who would believe it anyway? No one must know! Here is no ordinary picture. What do you think he would think if they all knew he was my lover?'

'Who?'

'*Il Cacciatore*, Mr Newman.'

James started to feel trapped. Déjà vu. But he must see it out.

'Our birth stamps our life,' she continued. 'If a duke is found to be a bastard he is a duke no longer. He cannot take his rightful place in the world as destiny has ordained.'

'I'm not quite sure I follow you.'

'Some people are very proud, Mr Newman. To some, pride is more important than life or death, certainly the lives of others anyway.'

She had run right off the rails. The poor maid.

'So, what you are saying to me is that you are willing to release the portrait for this international exhibition.'

'Yes, of course!'

'Thank you very much, Miss Turner. I know your attachment to my work...'

'My work!'

'Of course...and so I feel, more than anyone, I can fully appreciate the sacrifice you are making here.'

'No, you cannot!'

'Perhaps not. Anyway, thank you again. I will make all the necessary arrangements. Please trust me.'

So once again the portrait was hung with great acclaim ensuing. Miss Turner, or James, could not have asked for more. And again James's career was given an extra fillip by the fame, although to his disappointment he noticed one of his earlier technical fears beginning to be realised. The portrait was gradually breaking up, only in the background, however. The head remained immaculate. He had not noticed this in the dark of the Paddington flat, but under track-lights it was obvious and dispiriting. James wrote to Miss Turner detailing the deterioration and offering to do some gratis touch-up work. She replied that no one under any circumstances was to touch the painting, and stated unequivocally that this would be the very last time it would be lent out.

She was true to her word. Never again was the canvas to be seen. All entreaties to Miss Turner over the years fell on deaf ears and in time she was left alone, and in time almost forgotten. Not so the painting. It made James a minor international celebrity. He lost much of his shyness, and his manners and culture made him an extremely acceptable guest, James Newman, the painter of *Il Cacciatore*.

His mother died and he moved to Nice, retired to an eighteenth-century villa on an escarpment overlooking the Mediterranean. He left Sydney without much regret, but still occasionally browsed the *Herald* on the internet. On one of those nondescript matchless mornings that the Cote d'Azur seems to have in surplus, James spied a small item in the domestic news section: 'LOSS OF MASTERPIECE'.

With fearful premonition, he read on.

Firemen and police were called last night to Prince St, Paddington, where a large Victorian terrace house was severely gutted by fire. All occupants were evacuated safely except for an elderly paraplegic, a Miss Turner, owner of the house and occupier of the basement flat. Miss Turner is the owner of the famous painting *Il Cacciatore*, which appears to have been completely destroyed in the blaze. Conservation and art authorities described the double loss of house and painting as a 'tragedy'. Miss Turner is in a critical but stable condition in Prince of Wales Hospital with third-degree burns to eighty per cent of her body.

James was devastated. Completely destroyed! Unless Miss Turner had secreted it or something. Surely she would have tried to save her 'lover' before anything. What about the maid, presuming she was still around? No mention of her.

James rang up Peter Le Fevre. 'This is James here, James Newman.'

'James, it's half-past-fucking-three in the morning!'

'Yes, I'm sorry. Look, my painting, *Il Cacciatore*. I read about the fire on the internet.'

'Darling, I'm so sorry. I've been building up courage to ring you. There wasn't even a trace of it. The police have been working on some theory that the maid nicked it and set alight to the place, but after having seen her that hardly seems likely.'

'She was there?'

'Not "there" any longer. Mad as a cut snake. Babbling away. Couldn't understand a bloody word she said. Shock, apparent-ly. They've got her in the psychiatric ward at Prince of Wales.'

'Well, if there wasn't a trace, maybe the old duck managed to save it.'

'Well, she hasn't managed to save herself.'

'She's dead?'

'Not yet, but the doctors told me she shortly will be.'

'You've seen her.'

'Tried to…I had the same thoughts as you. Thought she might have hidden it or something, but they wouldn't let me in to speak to her. Apparently she's pretty far gone. That is, if it is her.'

'What are you talking about?'

'Well, it seems nobody's seen her for years. The tenants upstairs didn't know her and the estate agents haven't heard from her in ages. Maybe the maid had shacked up with someone. Maybe the painting wasn't even there. Who knows? When I asked to speak to your Miss Turner, the doctors told me I had the wrong person.'

'How would they know?'

'Search me.'

'I'm flying out.'

'Suit yourself.'

'I painted it. It's half mine.'

'Sure, sure. Well, good luck, James. See you soon.'

James booked, packed and, thirty-six hours later, in a heightened state of nervous and physical exhaustion, emerged into the bright glare and heat of an early Sydney summer. He flagged a cab to the hospital, leaving his luggage with the front desk who directed him to the psychiatric ward.

He couldn't find the charge nurse but a couple of nurses and most of the patients were sitting out on a long veranda in the sun. There were a few schizophrenic youths, but the ward was largely old people, some of whom were clearly ex-alcoholics. Patients were talking to themselves quietly, and an old lady next to James compulsively pulled fluff off her cardigan. They all seemed immensely depressed. He recognised Elspeth, even after the passing of years, sitting silently at the end of the group.

'Can I help you, sir?' One of the nurses approached him.

'Could I possibly have a word with that woman over there?'

'Elspeth Buchanan? I'll have to accompany you, sir. She's been through a traumatic experience. Elspeth, there's a man here to see you.'

No response. Elspeth was staring into space.

'Elspeth, do you remember me? It's James Newman, the painter.'

She looked up wildly into his eyes. 'Mr Newman!'

'Yes. Listen, Elspeth. It's very important. I want you to try and remember what happened to Miss Turner's picture, the one I painted, you remember? Were you still living with her? Was it destroyed in the fire?'

'*Il Cacciatore*!' Her eyes were wide with terror.

'Do you remember, Elspeth. Anything at all.'

She started to become agitated, then to shake. Finally she began to weep.

'Sir, I think it would be better if we left her alone for the present. She's not the best. The police have been here too, and another man. They had no success in talking to her. She doesn't remember, or she doesn't want to talk about it. Please, come along.'

'All right. Goodbye, Elspeth. Take care.'

She continued weeping, head in her hands.

The nurse led James back out into the main ward area.

A young man approached him, unnaturally thin with a fixed strained expression on his face. 'Do you know, mister?' he said. 'Everyone here is dead. Look at them. They're all rotting away.' His left hand was tightly closed. When he saw James notice this, the youth slowly opened it to reveal the head of a pigeon.

James stifled his revulsion and quickly moved on.

The front desk chased up the name on the computer. 'Marjorie Turner, did you say, sir?'

'Yes.'

'No, there's a Pamela Turner, a girl with a broken leg.'

'Maybe I have the wrong hospital. I wanted to speak to a woman who is a burn victim from a recent domestic fire in Paddington. She owned a famous painting, and I am the artist.'

'You are James Newman?'

'Did she mention me?'

'I read about it in the paper. There was a person taken from that fire, sir. They were up in the intensive care ward, but have just been transferred to the burns unit. They don't know who it is though. The victim is still unidentified.'

'It is her! Can I see her?'

'You will have to speak to the charge nurse, sir.'

James hurried up to the burns unit and unearthed the charge nurse, a stout saturnine matron in her late forties, a woman who no doubt had looked death in the face more than once.

'Would be possible for me to see the patient taken from the recent Paddington fire?'

'Are you a relative, sir?'

'I am an artist of an expensive portrait that the patient owned.'

'Right. Another man was here earlier and told me all about it. You've come from overseas?'

'I've just flown in. I know your patient is critical, but the work was very important for me, as you can imagine. I need to find out what happened to it.'

'I understand it was destroyed, sir, but you may see the patient now if you wish. It seems an extraordinary reversal has occurred in the condition.'

'Reversal?'

'A miracle, they say. One moment on the verge of death and now the doctors are talking about a complete recovery. I've never known the like.'

'Well, that is excellent. Can you take me to the room?'

'You will be allowed ten minutes only, sir.' She led him down a long corridor to a room at the very end. 'A visitor, nurse. Ten minutes.' She spoke brusquely to a girl sitting outside the room, browsing a magazine.

James opened the door and entered. A private room, large and sunny and silent. Lying on a high metal bed was a form entirely swathed in dressings. James felt a slight chill as he entered. He tentatively moved closer. 'Miss Turner, can you hear me? It's James Newman.'

The figure on the bed seemed to give a slight start. 'Mr Newman. I have heard so much about you. Tell me, where are you living at present?' The voice was low and strange, not recognisably her voice. Bizarrely, it also seemed to carry a slight continental accent.

'In France, Nice. Don't you remember my postcards? I've flown in to see you, my dear lady.'

'That is very kind of you, Mr Newman. When I am whole again, we must catch up. Don't forget to leave your address with me.'

'Miss Turner, I need to ask you about the painting.'

'The painting!'

James moved a little closer.

'Please do not come near!' the figure said abruptly, then more softly: 'You understand, Mr Newman, I do not want anyone to see me in this condition.'

'Yes, of course, but Miss Turner, I must know about the painting. Poor Elspeth cannot remember anything, it seems. She has gone into severe shock or something.'

'Elspeth is alive?' the figure spoke with sudden urgency. 'So she escaped! Where is she?'

'In the psychiatric ward. I've just seen her.'

'What did she say to you?' Again the urgent tone.

'Nothing at all. Look, Miss Turner, about the painting. Was it destroyed?'

This provoked a sardonic chuckle from the bed.

James was reaching the end of his tether. He moved right up.

'I asked you not to come near, Mr Newman!'

'But I must know. Why all these questions? Why don't you just tell me, for Christ's sake!'

'For Christ's sake,' the figure repeated. Such a large head, it must be her.

He looked down at that bandaged head into the only visible physical feature, the eyes. Suddenly he seized up. A terrific fear clutched him. He looked deeply into those eyes, thunderstruck for a few seconds, then raced from the room, frantic.

He paused for breath halfway down the stairway. What had he seen? It was madness, impossible! His heart thumped against his ribs. It just could not be! He was overtired, overwrought. He turned to go back into the room, but fear held him and stopped him. He could not go back. He could never face that form again. He descended the stairs groggily, collected his luggage, and out the front door without acknowledging the duty nurse hailing him from the counter. He took a cab directly to the airport.

There was no flight to Paris for twenty-four hours. He was exhausted. Perhaps he should book into a hotel. No, he'd never sleep. He didn't want to leave the airport. He never wanted to step into the country again.

The hours dragged by, achingly. He dozed as best he could on the overlarge lounges and flicked through inane magazines. He nibbled tasteless cafeteria food, resisted a strong temptation to drink, and spent the night in a feverish nervous stupor on a chair in a protected corner. There were a few others around. He made sure of that. Every little noise now startled him.

Finally grey day came. He still had to wait until two in the afternoon. It was the longest time he had ever known. He paced the length of the terminal anxiously. All around were people wishing joyful bon voyages or receiving their loved ones with tears and hugs. Another world.

Finally, the hour came round. He stood in the departure lounge, smoking his umpteenth packet. They called his flight. This was it. He was going.

Someone was calling his name. He swung round. It was Peter Le Fevre.

Peter ran up to him breathlessly and grabbed him.

'James. My God, you look awful! At last I've found you! I've been looking all over. You wouldn't believe. Listen, James, something terrible has happened. I don't understand it but I had to find you and tell you.'

'What?'

'That Turner woman's maid.'

'Elspeth? What about her?'

'Murdered, James, brutally murdered. A horrible death. Found in one of the hospital toilets, bludgeoned by some madman to a bloody pulp.'

A profound chill ran down James's spine. 'Some madman. Do the police have any leads?'

'Nothing at all. They came to me completely mystified. I told them all I could, which is nothing. James, something weird is happening, isn't it? Something's very wrong. That picture was so valuable. You just appeared with it one day out of the blue. James, is your life in danger? Do you know?'

'I don't know… but I think so.'

The last call for the flight came over the intercom.

'James, tell me what is happening.'

'I don't know. It's all so crazy. Look, Peter, once I'm on the plane I'll be right. I'll be away from this place.'

'OK, but take care. Take care for Christ's sake.'

'For Christ's sake. Yes, Peter, I promise you, I'll take care.'

They embraced. James picked up his hand luggage and proceeded down the enclosed gangway and onto the plane. He walked up and down both aisles and looked at every single face but did not recognise a soul. He seated himself, buckled up, and waited. The safety precautions were read out; then the plane turned, taxied down the runway, accelerated, and lifted off. He was away. He had escaped.

They rose high up over the ocean then banked and headed north-west. Through his window James saw the numberless red roofs of the suburbs, then the plane swung over Sydney Harbour and he bid a silent permanent farewell to the miniature Bridge and Opera House, the white curves of the beaches and the wide glittering blue of the Pacific. Relief of mind led his body at last to relaxation and he slumped into a long, deep sleep as the plane pushed slowly back to the old world.

Nice was as he had left it and James settled back into the established rhythm of his new life, although not completely. Something, he hardly knew what, kept disturbing his peace of mind. He became increasingly restless during the day and found it difficult to sleep at night and, as an unsettled autumn turned to an unusually icy winter, he fell into a kind of cold nervous reverie.

He was now possessed, continually, by an odd and singular mood. He knew he had felt like this at some point in the past, but could not remember when. This sense of déjà vu added to the strangeness of the whole business.

Then, one night, it came to him in a dream and he awoke with a shock. He had felt the same as this that autumn, many years ago, just before he had painted the Turner portrait. And it was almost exactly the same time of year. Maybe that was partly it; he was locked into a universal sense of shifting unreality. Or maybe he was just getting old. No, it was something stronger than that, far more distinctive and assertive.

He tried to recall that time, the details, the fitful weather, the long melancholy walks through the paper-barks in Centennial Park, caustic Molière at The Wharf, and that odd dead dog. That season, of course, was not as severe as its counterpart here. Here was a real winter coming on, wild and bitter. James could see from his house huge storms beating up from the ocean, the rain hurtling down and black waves crashing over the sea walls protecting the road below. He had never known storms like these, uncontrollable entities that had somehow smashed their way through the Pillars of Hercules.

The season wore on, increasingly ferocious. James lay awake at night, alert and expectant, while rain and hail lashed his house and the wind moaned in the old defunct chimney.

One night he lay there, preternaturally alive to every sound. A storm raged without, yet still he could hear the ticking of the mantelpiece clock downstairs and the odd mouse scurrying over the floorboards.

Suddenly from outside and amidst the storm, there was the most heart-rending cry for help. *'Au secours! Au secours!'* it rang out, over and over.

James sat bolt upright in his bed. It sounded like a woman, but it was at such a pitch he could not be sure. He strained every sense with utmost alertness out towards the night, but now he could hear only the storm. Maybe he had dreamt it. My God, how furious the wind was! He turned to settle down.

There were three bold knocks on the door. He sat up again. Could it be the storm? They sounded so definite, but who would be abroad on such a night, and why? Nothing.

Then the scream rang out again piercing the wild night. *'Au secours! Au secours!'* This time it was louder, more insistent and more urgent.

Nothing again, and then, as if on cue, the three knocks, stronger.

Yes, this time there was no mistake. Someone was outside his front door. But who? Someone in distress. James was terrified, but why? It was just his bloody nerves. Someone was in distress, clearly. It was his duty to help. He must try and help.

He rose and donned a greatcoat and a pair of wellingtons. He flicked on the lights and descended the stairs into the hall. He paused, hesitant, and for some peculiar reason he then asked himself what it was that had most delighted him in life. The answer came clearly: it was his love of painting children, unconsciously reflecting his own essential unsmirched innocence.

Then the huge knocks rang out again and again through the house above the noise of the storm. Who was on the other side of that door?

James advanced deliberately, and as he did a weird feeling of compulsion overtook him. With each successive step, he felt more driven to approach that door and open it. A sense of predestination, of ordainment, never before had James Newman felt so sure about the necessity of a particular action. He drew back the bolt and turned the handle. It was roughly wrenched from his grasp and his fate embraced him.

An Unexpected Meeting

Another depressing visit with Mum at the home. All that endless shit; she just can't let it go. In fact, seems increasingly determined to hang on to it. Pain is life, when there's nothing else. Still, there are good and bad days. The rages are less frequent, or so the duty nurse says. God, how she used to bang Cheryl around as a kid! Of course nothing like the old man used to bang them both around. Still gives her nightmares, tearing wildly down the yard, huddling behind the shed with the other vermin. Miserable prick he was. Never got his comeuppance. They never do. And Cheryl never found the guts to face him as she always told herself she would. Just walked away one fine cold morning, the sun on her face, calling from afar. Left them to it, and the grog.

A day very like today, the sky such an intense winter blue, maybe a little gardening if her joints are up to it. Checks the letter box. Daddy-long-legs. She re-latches the gate in the high stone wall behind her. Her sanctuary. And she is face to face with the biggest man she has ever seen in her life, huge, the proverbial brick shithouse. Stale acrid smell of alcohol and sweat, nothing on his feet, despite the season, a pair of stained stubbies and an old footie jumper; and on both his bulging shoulders two cardboard boxes, one containing her television set and video player, the other her computer, screen and printer. The various flexes dangle idly in the air. He stands there stock still, returning her stare.

Time ticks by.

Finally he says, 'Harry asked me…told me…you wanted all this stuff taken over to the new place. Yeah, yeah, that's it.'

More eyeballing. Her mind is racing. She must reply.

'That's right. Harry did say that. But now I've changed my mind and I'd like it left back where it was, thank you very much.'

Another pause in proceedings. Cheryl becomes hyper-aware of the lorikeets chirriping wildly in the bottlebrush down the back corner of the yard. She must keep her eyes on him.

'Righto then, I'll just take it all back inside.'

'If you wouldn't mind.'

'No worries, love.'

He smiles briefly, no top teeth, then turns and starts back up the garden path, past the roses, past the hydrangeas. And for some unaccountable reason, Cheryl follows in his large masculine shadow. They reach the front door, or what was the front door. One of the hinges is still hanging on and that's about it. They both step gingerly over the splinters and enter the living room, which also looks like it's been hit by a bomb. Only the wallpaper has survived, which needed replacing anyway. Books, CDs, lamps, the Royal Doulton, the rubber plant's been booted out of its pot, the chairs are all broken, the lounge, the bookcase…

She walks around looking at it all, dazed. Meanwhile, his lordship just stands there, in the middle of the room, boxes still on his shoulders. What to say? What to do? A flash of inspiration.

She turns, looks him squarely in the eyes and musters all the amazement in her voice she can manage, 'My God, look at this, I've been robbed!'

He considers this for a while. His face reddens, then clears, and he opens his eyes as wide as a child's. 'Why fuck me dead, ma'am, so you have!'

So far, so good. What next? She starts to lose her nerve. Her mum always says when you've got to act, you should never think too much, but she's thinking madly, can't stop herself:

Cheryl, what do your possessions matter? What matters is your safety, what matters is you, so why on earth did you follow this man into your house? Just look at the mess he's made, the destruction, that presumably nobody heard. And why did he waste his time and energy doing that? Because he's

*violent. He enjoys it. He's a big violent man who has been caught committing
a crime by you, against you, and here you are, here I am in the same room
with him with no one around, surrounded by a house, a garden and a high
wall. I could scream, of course, but he'd probably knock me senseless in a
moment. Actually, he could do what he liked with me right now, knock me
out, tie me up, take the stuff anyway. He could even rape me if he has the
mind to it. Would he rape me? I'm no oil painting, God knows, but as far as
I know, that doesn't matter much to rapists. I've always considered that being
robbed, or beaten, or raped, were things that happened to other people, people
like my mum, people in the paper or on the telly. And here I am, suddenly one
of these same people. Come on, snap out of it. He's not making any violent
moves, or any moves at all for that matter, just standing in the middle of the
room with the boxes on his shoulders.*

She's got to do, say, something, keep some kind of handle on the
situation. But what? She looks him in the face again and sees that he is
waiting for her, expecting her to make a move, maybe even take his cue
from her. 'You can put the boxes down now, if you like.'

'Thank you, ma'am, they was getting a bit heavy.'

He places them down swiftly, cleanly, as though they weigh nothing,
are full of feathers and not her heavy re-saleable possessions. Then all
at once he begins to get fidgety, scratching at his three-day growth and
glancing around the room at his handiwork; then rubbing his hands
together and rolling his eyes, as though he wants to do something but
can't figure out what it is.

Cheryl tries to speak again but nothing comes out, just a strange
croak. He starts to look at her nervously, wondering what she's up to,
and then he starts to look a little ugly, and she knows she's got to speak.

'I suppose you've got a few things you want to be doing today.'

It seems to her that somebody else has just said that. She's having
some sort of out-of-body experience, watching herself, listening to
herself. She's not going to be able to hang on like this much longer.
And at this point he bends down and picks up one of the legs of the
chairs lying conveniently near his left foot. He picks it up without

actually looking at it, as though he knew it was there all along, he stood in that exact spot on purpose, and he starts lightly tapping his leg with it. Tap, tap, tap. Then he holds it up and has a good look at it, takes a few swings through the air, just to gauge its heft she supposes, check if it's what he wants, what he needs. She is freaking out watching this, but not moving a muscle, not making any sound.

'Things? Yeah, I do have a few things to do as a matter of fact.'

He takes a few more air swings and takes a little step towards her, smiles slightly, but this time without parting his lips. 'So, I guess I'd better be moving along, that right, ma'am?'

Now I'm caught between relief and terror, wondering what he actually means, cause he doesn't move, just taps the chair leg on his hand, tap, tap, tap, then grips its foot, and rolls his eyes a bit more, and then he begins to look ugly again, but really ugly, and I just cannot do or say a bloody thing, just stand there and look at him. I can see he's really tossing over the situation now, considering his various options, and he's looking worse and worse, tapping that chair leg in his hand a little faster, he starts to shake a bit, like he's going to have a fit or something, break out, he's breathing heavily too, I try not to notice, and I don't even think I can even scream any more. I always wondered why some people never scream in these situations, and now I'm just like that myself, then all at once he…

He relaxes, just relaxes, and gives her a big cheesy toothless grin. 'Well, ma'am, it's been a pleasure.'

She nods, or something like, tries to smile, and he backs slowly towards the doorway, but when he reaches the doorway, he stops and turns around, regards his carpentry, and says thickly, 'You know, you oughta get yourself a proper door. These ones, they're as weak as piss… ma'am.'

She nods again, and he says, 'Righto, well, see you later, I guess.'

He ambles back down the path, as though he's out on an evening stroll, even breaks into a tuneless whistle, gives her a jaunty wave from the gate with the chair leg, shuts the gate carefully behind him, and he's gone.

Night Prey

Parker was in a nightclub up at the Cross, past midnight, with an army mate and his girl. There was a live band, good, but it wasn't the right mood for dancing, so he just leant back with them in the corner, beers and joints, watching and listening. Silent, friendly company.

The band took a break and Parker's mate asked him if he'd like to feel the music a bit, pulling out of the top pocket of his flak jacket a small plastic cache of white powder. Parker licked his finger, dipped it in, rubbed the incredibly bitter stuff around his gums and sucked his finger clean.

Another beer and it started to work, just as his mate had said, through the music. Before, the music had been hammering him, but now it was if it was coming out of himself, especially the beat. He got up and danced, lost it for a while, then went to look for a toilet, following a barman's directions through two heavy swinging glass doors and down a long flight of stairs.

As soon as those doors flapped closed behind him, Parker entered another world. The music was far away. He walked down the stairs, and at the bottom took a long corridor to the left, brown-painted concrete walls with moisture dripping down and a floor covered in stained brown lino curling at the edges with damp. This led to another similar corridor, again leading to the left, and this finally to the toilet. He pushed open a small raised door, also heavy, and entered a blaze of white.

The room was long and large and clad entirely in shiny white tiles, except the ceiling, which was painted in white gloss and from which shone four bright strip lights. One of these flickered intermittently.

The silver stainless-steel urinal ran entirely along one side, wall to wall. Everything was designed, calculated, to convey an impression of sterility. For some reason, Parker had lost the urge to piss. He stood there a while but nothing came. Perhaps sensing the warmth of his body, water suddenly flushed down with roaring violence, then shut off. He zipped up his pants.

He began to feel a little strange. He couldn't hear the music, couldn't hear anything except the uneven drilling buzz of the flickering light. He had money on him, not a large amount, but enough. And here he was in this enormous fucking white room, far removed from anyone, with one small door for entry and exit. So what if some shithead had seen him stumbling drunkenly down to the toilet and followed him? There were plenty of them around. What if one or two or more of them were padding right now along that greasy lino intending to bash and rob him? What if they burst in? What could he do? His screams couldn't be heard. There was only one escape and they would block it. They might do anything, taunt him, slap him around, bash him slowly to bloody death. No one would know. He looked very straight with his army haircut, almost like a pig. That alone would be sufficient to provoke them, and the money sufficient to make sure he didn't follow them out. The bright red of his blood against the shiny white of the tiles. Why was he such a fool to let himself get caught in such a place with all this money? He should have known better. He had to get out while there was still time.

Slowly he edged towards the door and, bracing himself, with both hands quickly quietly pulled it open. A blank corridor with a blank end. He padded swiftly and silently in semi-crouch along the lino, paused at the corner and furtively looked around. He could see the foot of the stairs at the very end of the corridor. He bolted along the corridor back up the stairs and into the warmth, bustle and noise which overwhelmed him, swept right through him. That huge warm pulse. So this world was still here, incredible, just as he had left it, like he'd never gone. He weaved his way back to his seat.

Meanwhile, his mate had struck up a conversation with three business types, still in their suits at this time of night. The girlfriend had drifted off somewhere. These blokes were drunk and had just come from a function up on Oxford Street. They were boasting how they had walked down here through some sort of no-man's land between Oxford Street and the Cross.

You've got to understand that that part of Sydney in those days, late sixties, what with the R & R and all the money and drugs and hookers and everything else was pretty violent, especially the area just south of the Cross where Darlinghurst turns to Paddington. Even the pigs, who had their collective fingers in all sorts of pies, left the area well alone, and it had quickly gained a colourful notoriety. The coppers were always warning the public, on the quiet, not to walk, or even drive through the twisting narrow maze of lanes and streets at night. And this was where these blokes had just walked through.

All three had smooth-shaven shiny drunken faces, horrible in their way, flushed with the night air. They were gabbling and laughing with relief and bravado. One of them, a fat Rotarian type, with a face like a pig too, but pale, very pale, intense and empty, Parker had seen the type hundreds of times before, just started speaking straight at him.

'Mate, we saw nothing, nothing at all.' He rubbed the pad of his open palm into his left eye over and over, which really got on Parker's nerves. 'I don't know where all the bloody gangs were. We walked straight through, straight through, and nobody laid a finger on us, not a fucking finger, didn't see a soul. If we can do it, why can't the coppers? Lazy bastards.'

The band started up again and conversation became impossible. Parker sat back and drank some more beer and just let his head spin.

He left a few hours later. He was drunk but very alert. He lived then at Surry Hills. The buses had long stopped running and, as usual, he'd spent all his money on drink for himself and others, but anyway the walk home would do him no harm. The no-man's land the two businessmen had traversed lay between the Cross and his home. He always skirted around it, walking down William Street. He walked up Bayswater Road to the heart of the Cross, battled through the crowd lit up in the unearthly fire-glow of the neon, all their faces also looked intense and empty, then crossed the road in front of the old Darlinghurst police station which stood on the edge of the reputedly forbidden and dangerous area.

As he crossed the road, Parker noticed the dark ends of the streets that wound their way eventually up to Taylor Square, like a network of nerves. What went on in those streets at night, he wondered? Where did they lead and who was in them? Those businessmen had walked through and nothing had happened, they hadn't even seen a single person. Why shouldn't he do the same? It would shorten his journey. Presumably ordinary people lived in the area and they walked in and out day by day. So without further consideration he plunged up an alley pointing in the general direction of Taylor Square.

Almost immediately he noticed how dark it was away from the lights of the Cross. Very dark, very quickly. The few streetlights were out for some reason. There were no lights on in any windows, what little light there was did not come from the houses but from their old leaning walls, and also, weirdly, from the asphalt beneath his feet. The grey curtains in the windows looked as if they were carved from stone. Then, just for a moment, the houses all became a sinister mask. He began to imagine the violent dramas, domestic and criminal, that had over the years been enacted in these houses and presently vacant lanes. These grey blank vistas. A scream would go nowhere, sink right into the ground with all the blood and pain and horror.

The houses, the street; he saw what he needed to do was reduce these things to their ordinariness, their banality. Yet strangely, when he focused seriously upon it, it was the very idea of their ordinariness that he seemed to find so unsettling. Perhaps because he did not belong here.

The lane he was following ran about a hundred yards, then split into two smaller lanes that both ran off at odd angles. He chose the right. He couldn't see the end of this street, not only because of the dark, but also – a thing he became conscious of only after some time – the street was slowly curving around. He walked right in the centre of the cracked asphalt. There was hardly any footpath and what footpath there was, was smashed up and cluttered with rusted tins and weeds and other rubbish. The houses were all two and three-storeyed terraces in a continual wall, old, uniform and decaying. It seemed that all of them must have been derelict because he passed no lights, or any sign of habitation whatever. There was no one on the streets. He was alone. His footsteps did not echo but were immediately swallowed by the dark. There was no movement of air. It seemed slightly warmer here than in the Cross, although it was not particularly hot or cold. The air was musty, close, but there were no strong smells, smells of life.

Parker felt with the constant curve of the road he was probably now heading in the wrong direction. A laneway offered itself on the left and he took it. He walked along for a while but this lane also seemed to curve. There were no street signs and all the streets looked exactly the same.

Then he thought he heard something behind him. He stopped and looked around. The empty street, the leaning houses. He listened. Nothing, only his own breathing. The silence oppressed him, and a strange feeling of apprehension began slowly to creep over him. Now for some reason the air seemed more dense, as though with a suppressed expectation, a sort of gathering. He shivered, although he was not cold.

He was getting lost, he didn't know the way and apparently it wasn't easy to find the way. But he hadn't gone very far, so perhaps it would be better if he retraced his steps and returned to the Cross. He turned around and started walking back. He came to the beginning of the lane, turned right and continued along expecting at any moment to find the original fork. It must have been further than he thought.

It began to seem interminable, and just when he felt this, again Parker thought he heard something behind him. He stopped and turned around. The empty street, the leaning houses. Perhaps the person or cat or whatever was just beyond the curve in the road, always keeping out of sight. Nothing necessarily sinister, although why would they do that? Holding his breath, he crept back silently fifty yards. Nothing unusual to be seen at all. He turned around and walked on.

But the road never seemed to lead to the original fork. He must have made a mistake. He stopped to think, but couldn't work out where he'd gone wrong. He went on further, then took another laneway to the left leading in what he felt sure must be the direction of the Cross but this just led to another fork. This wasn't the original fork because he couldn't see any light at the end of one of the ways. It seemed now he was completely lost. He stood quietly and thought about it in a calm and clear-headed fashion, drawing on his training. Taylor Square lay on higher ground than the Cross. Perhaps he could find his way by following the inclination of the land. There was a lane to the right that seemed to slope steadily upwards. There was none to the left. He resolved to return to his original intention and push up to Taylor Square. Because of the slope of this lane, Parker felt confident it would take him in the right direction. He turned along it and started to feel better as he continued uphill. He was now tired but surely sooner or later he must come to a major thoroughfare.

Ever since his first tour in Vietnam, Parker had been prey to a strange recurring nightmare, which he could never remember when awake, although each time it came upon him when asleep he remembered having had it before. For some reason, just at that moment, the memory of this nightmare, for the first time, flooded fully into his conscious mind.

He is alone and lost in a jungle wilderness amongst the ridges of some wild inaccessible mountain chain in enemy territory. Following a track that runs steadily upwards, but because the foliage on either side is high and thick, he never has any view as to where he is. With all his gear he trudges for hours and hours knowing that sooner or later the gradient will have to change, he can't keep going up forever. When it does change, then he knows he's over the mountains, finally, and on safe ground again. But nothing ever seems to change at all. He keeps walking at exactly the same inclination. He wearies in the muddy heat and at last decides to ditch his pack. After this he continues a little brighter in spirits for the new lightness in his step. Again he walks for what seems like an interminably long period. He loses all sense of time and grows more exhausted. At last he sees an object on the track ahead. He wonders what it could possibly be and hurries towards it, hoping it will give him some clue as to his whereabouts. As he approaches it, he realises with amazement that it is his pack which he has dropped so many miles back. This is impossible. It's impossible he's been going around in circles because he's been walking upwards the whole time. Then with great horror the truth flashes: he has been walking around the inside of the world, thinking he was climbing, but simply returning again and again on his tracks. Then there is a brief hallucinatory image of the world as his skull and there the dream ends. He doesn't know what any of this means, nor why the dream came consciously to him at that particular moment.

Up all along he toiled and toiled. Then, for a third time, he thought he heard something behind him. He stopped and peered back into the murk but, predictably, faced the same unchanged unchanging prospect. No! He was convinced the perspective had altered, slightly, subtly. But how? What? He peered closely but couldn't tell. Nevertheless, he knew, for a surety, it was different.

He was completely lost, miles from anywhere, or anyone. What if somebody really was tracking him, maybe the same person or persons he sensed while in the toilet? He had no money left but they weren't to know this. Maybe they'd watched his lavish spending back at the nightclub. He was tired and drunk and drugged and couldn't properly defend himself. But then why hadn't this presence declared itself. There'd been plenty of time and opportunity. What were they waiting for? Accomplices? Or were they just enjoying the game? All Parker could really do was ignore them. He looked ahead. The road ran on steadily upwards. Surely he would come to Taylor Square soon. He hurried on.

Now he knew someone or something was pursuing him, stalking him, he needed to hurry faster and faster towards safety. He had reached an almost frantic state when finally he saw a T-intersection ahead. He raced towards it and, to his relief, saw that the lane he had been following ran into a much larger road. Strangely, though, when he reached this road, it was also completely empty. It ran along flat left and right. Without consideration he turned right.

He maintained his pace; to do so seemed to him to be essential. Once he betrayed a falling off, he was done, they would move in. This road surely would lead somewhere, he must be nearing Taylor Square. Parker was again aware of something at his back, but this time there really was something, it was not a noise, but a light. He turned around. Two lights, car headlights. He walked on. The lights grew larger, but strangely, he suddenly realised he could hear no accompanying noise of a motor. Something was wrong. He turned back around and saw with a shock the headlights now entirely spanning the width of the road. They grew larger as he watched. His scalp pricked and his body turned to ice. The vehicle was trying to run him down. He turned and ran, and as he ran the road began to slope downwards, catapulting him forwards faster and faster. The light grew larger at his back. He dared not look around. Then he saw a salvation. There was a little lane to the right just ahead. If only he could reach it in time. He sprinted wildly and just managed to dart into the lane as the vehicle swept noiselessly past.

He leant against a damp wall of one of the empty houses panting with relief. After a while, he looked out onto the road again. It was clear. Parker decided to follow the lane that he had entered as it also ran steadily upwards.

He walked on for what again seemed like hours and at last emerged onto another empty major road. Surely he would be more successful this time. He turned to the right again and started to walk along the wide level way.

He hurried along, knowing he was again being followed. Again at his back he sensed a light. Fear slid into his bones. He turned around. Two headlights, and obviously they were coming at him more quickly than before. He sprinted. The light grew larger and larger behind him at a seemingly uncontrollable rate. He focused on running as fast as he possibly could, looking around desperately for any escape. Again the road started to slope steeply downwards.

The vehicle was almost upon him. There was a lane again to the right just ahead. He couldn't reach it. The vehicle was about to hit. He dived headlong and scrambled into the lane. The vehicle rushed by noiselessly.

Parker lay prostrate in the lane, exhausted, seized up, unable to think or move. What was happening to him? What was going to happen? He just lay there, the damp rocky road imprinting his face and the stinking soil in his mouth.

At length he regained some composure and recovered his breath. He rolled over, sat up, spat, then stood stiffly and brushed himself down. His palms were bloody and his knees and one hip were grazed through his trousers, which were ruined, but basically he was unhurt.

He ventured back out onto the road, which was empty. He couldn't work out how he'd managed to catch up with the strange vehicle a second time. It must have stopped and he'd passed it somehow on a back road. It seemed to be travelling in a consistent direction. He decided that if he walked up the road instead of down, there could be no chance of him coming across it again. A road of this size must lead somewhere, but where? And also where were the people, and the other cars? It was a late hour, but still…

He continued slowly up the wide road. By now he was exhausted and his steps were unsteady. He forced himself to press on. He wanted to lie down but knew he could not stop here. Something told him that to do so would mean death or incredible horror or pain. Sooner or later he must come out onto a main road, or it would get light, or something. He still couldn't shake off the feeling he was being pursued, and when, for a moment, he tried to consider this rationally, for the third time, he sensed the light behind him.

He turned around. The vehicle again, but how? He broke into a mad run, but hopelessly, because this time he knew there would be no lanes to escape into and he had no time to make the one he'd left. Furthermore, he was running uphill. The vehicle was coming up quickly upon him. He laboured frantically, fear driving him well beyond what he thought was his endurance. He gasped for breath and drove and drove himself, but this time he knew there was no escape. Still he pushed himself on. The houses on either side seemed to be coming together. Then they were suddenly, glaringly, terrifyingly illuminated by the headlights. It was hopeless, he was lost, the vehicle was here, upon him already, so quickly, too quickly, no escape, the light was monstrous, terror was upon him, he was aware of nothing else, terror, and then just as he felt the vehicle about to strike, Parker screamed, and as he screamed, there came flashing into his mind a vision of a large sterile room with six white shiny surfaces, silent, empty and waiting. He was on the point of agonising death, but somehow he sensed another escape to his right and instinctively dived at it.

He scrambled madly on his hands and knees then on his feet up a laneway and all at once burst into the bright lights and bustle of Taylor Square. He slumped onto the footpath and wept, then vomited over his pants and shoes. Breathless, he sat back, unable to move, dazed, sweat tricking down his face. The few people still wandering past at that hour avoided him. Cars and buses swished by, also indifferent.

He remained in that same position for an unaccountable time, then finally, as the eastern sky lightened to ash, picked himself up and limped home.

The Shark

Jane's first impression of Birra was of an idyll. Her little Laser rounded a sharp bend and suddenly she fronted a panorama of almost cloying beauty. She pulled over onto the gravelly verge, unclipped her seat belt, unfolded herself out of the driver's door and stretched out her right foot, which was stiff and sore from the accelerator. It had been a long drive.

From beneath the headland of massive sea-strewn boulders on which her car was parked, the silky white ribbon of Ten Mile Beach swept away into the distance up to Cape Byron and its lighthouse, which flashed periodically through a penumbra of sea mist. A heavy tropical storm had just marched through, she watched its solid mass receding to the north-east over the ocean, and the air was still threateningly dark and dense although it was only mid-afternoon.

The township, newly rinsed, nestled prettily behind the low tropical scrub that backed the beach dune. Behind this were orderly farms and muddy brown rivers snaking their way through mangrove swamps, and behind these rose the rainforested mountains of far north New South Wales with mists rising off them like steam, up towards big black clouds and bright breaks of hot sky. She could clearly discern Mount Warning; its stark height and bulk dominated the horizon, just as Captain James Cook must have seen it over two hundred years ago as his ship *Endeavour*, somewhere near here, veered perilously close to destruction.

She considered a photo, decided against, she was not a tourist after all, then eased herself back into the bucket seat. Here at last, the days of the dole behind her and her career ahead. It all hadn't really struck her till now, actually sighting the place, being here.

She was lucky to be offered the position. Her grades had been good but there was no shortage of unemployed teachers. Such a relief to shed Social Security and the inner-city cramp of MacDonaldtown. Jane was sorry to leave her housemates; she and Janine and Susan had all done their DipEd together, hung out, listened to music, watched films. It had been fun, but she was eager to work. She had always seen herself as a teacher, and would have been quite willing to start off somewhere totally remote and gradually work her way back to Sydney over the years. But this was an unexpected boon, although the official who had interviewed her at the Department of Education had told her the town was not a happy one.

It seemed eerily quiet as she drove through the outskirts, the streets empty, a quiet more like that before than after a storm. This was big-city neurosis, no doubt. It would be strange adjusting to such a slower pace. Even life on the dole in Sydney, ironically, seemed more hyped-up than the prospect of working fulltime in a country town. No more living off her nerves in hip late-night cafés on King Street. Instead, easy-going ways, friendliness, honesty, trust and a real sense of community. The conservatism would annoy her but this would be well offset by the lifestyle. The rent was cheap, the beaches would be uncrowded and the water unpolluted. Sydney was eight hours away, too far for a weekend drive, but her friends had promised to travel up and stay with her. The school was small, no more than thirty pupils, so she could get to know them all personally.

She cruised down the wide main street. Still not a soul in sight. But it all looked as it should: deep gutters with old muddy utes parked rear to curb, red water still gurgling furiously down the drains, carious double-storeyed Victorian pubs with filigreed wrought-iron balconies, the Palladian facade of the Commonwealth Bank, the neo-Gothic council chambers, wooden general stores and odd specialty shops. She noticed wherever there was a gap, weeds proliferated, and all structures, grand and humble, had peeling paintwork and were roofed in rusty corrugated iron.

Jane had been offered the flat of the former teacher for the area, Mr

Simmons, who had gone bush or something, she couldn't quite get the story straight from the Department of Education, which didn't own the place but had some unorthodox arrangement with the man who did, a Mr Jeffries, living with his wife downstairs. Slightly strange set-up, but she supposed up here the rule book held less sway than convenience and established procedure, and it also saved her the trouble of scouting around. If it didn't suit, she could always move.

The flat was in Bond Street, which she spotted on her left a couple of blocks beyond the town centre, number seventeen. She slowed to first. The street was neat, although there was no curb and gutter, modest bungalows set well back behind luxuriant gardens. Her place was closer to the street and somewhat isolated, a straight up and down brick box, typically fifties, the type of building and design that had so blighted the suburbs of Sydney.

She parked, slipped past a gate hanging off its hinges, and rapped ineffectually on the fly-screen door. 'Hello? Anyone home?'

'Just a tick!' A booming contralto resounded from the interior. Its owner emerged from the corridor gloom and flung the door open, almost striking Jane in the face, an enormous middle-aged woman in a bright floral dress girdled with a pink apron.

'What can I do for you, love?'

'I'm Jane Spencer. I believe I'm renting the flat upstairs.'

'You're the new chalkie. Goodo. Been wondering where you'd got to. I'm Mrs Jeffries. Me husband's the landlord. Pleased to meet you.' Mrs Jeffries grasped Jane's hand in a grip of iron.

'Charmed.' Jane fought back tears. The woman's right arm was like a pair of thick sausages, the flesh dimpled but firm. Her underarms were unshaven and their odour pierced right to the back of Jane's sinuses. Significantly overweight, obese even, but she seemed to be very much in the full vigour of life. Probably about fifty, a coarse kindly face, sunburnt red, with a snub nose and a pair of bright blue eyes set like buttons.

'I guess you been driving for hours.'

'Yes, I have actually.'

'Well, leave your clobber for now and come and have a cuppa.'

'Only if you're making one…'

'Love, I'm always making one.' She laughed heartily, ending in a small fit of wheezing.

'That would be very nice.'

Jane followed her down the corridor into a musty living room, full of junk. The blinds were drawn against the sun and it took a few moments for Jane's eyes to adjust to the twilight. There was a huge old radiogram taking up most of one wall and a crazy assortment of shabby armchairs upon one of which lounged a moth-eaten cattle dog which paid her no heed. Innumerable tea-rings patterned all wooden surfaces.

'Jim ain't in. He's workin'. Have a seat, make yourself at home. I'll be back in a jiffy.'

She swept from the room and Jane subsided into a chair from which she felt she might have some difficulty extracting herself. The dog was snoring audibly and fouling the air.

Presently Mrs Jeffries returned with a pot of tea brewed to the consistency of mud accompanied by some rock-hard scones. Still, Jane accepted these gratefully, both for the hospitality they denoted and also because after her drive she was hungry and thirsty.

'What line of work is your husband in?'

'Line of work…that's a good one. Well, he used to be a cane-cutter, love, like most menfolk round here, but when that fell through Henry Jacobson down at the garage was kind enough to offer him a few odd jobs. I do a bit of washin' and ironin' meself. All helps to make ends meet.'

'I've never lived in the country before. I hope I fit in without too much trouble.'

'You'll be all right. Come to the club with us on Saturday night and meet a few folks.'

'I will. Thank you.'

'You'll have no worries. Far as we're all concerned, there's no way you could be half as bad as the bloke yer replacin'.'

'Yes…what happened to him?'

'Fell in with bad company. Don't you worry your pretty little head about that.'

This last statement irritated Jane, but as it was delivered in a flat tone of finality she let it hang. She changed the subject and they chatted on amiably, but rather awkwardly. Mrs Jeffries was so country!

When the small talk petered out, Mrs Jeffries took Jane upstairs and showed her the flat, which seemed satisfactory, cleaner and brighter in fact than Mrs Jeffries's own place.

As they descended the wooden steps it began to rain, big fat drops.

'Better get your stuff in, love. Looks like another storm's brewin'. I'll give you a hand.'

The sky did look ominous. Jane hurried down to the car and with Mrs Jeffries's help had everything inside her flat in a few minutes. She had not brought much. They were just in time. On the last trip, the heavens opened with a roar, drenching poor Jane as she struggled up.

'You'll have to get used to that, love. Up here it comes down like that all the time. Rain and shine, rain and shine, it's like a bloomin' circus.' Mrs Jeffries smiled and shook her head good-naturedly. 'I'll leave you to it. Reckon you got a bit to sort out. If you need anything, give us a yell.' With that, she was gone, out into the storm.

Jane stood at a loss for a moment, in an unfamiliar place with her personal items scattered about in haphazard heaps. She walked over to the back window and let up the blind. It looked out onto a small square yard, bare except for the mandatory rotary Hills hoist positioned dead centre. Washing was still hanging from it, sagging, in the pouring rain. It looked so glum, she felt flat, drained of energy. Just tiredness. With an effort of will she pulled herself together, and set to unpacking and making her new home. While she worked she could hear the water thundering all around.

Australia in the mid-eighties, the nation approaching its bicentenary, and Jane Spencer, like most, very much of her class and time. Born in 1964 in Bexley, a nondescript middle-class suburb, and raised there, the only child of a settled suburban solicitor and a dedicated housewife. Educated at the local Church of England Girls Grammar School followed by a Bachelor of Arts at Sydney University. She'd had a precious and somewhat lonely childhood, enjoying the luxury of developing strong personal opinions and having them indulged rather than challenged, although she had a somewhat distant, even formal relationship with both her parents, as indeed, it seemed to Jane, they had with one another. Birra was her first time away from Sydney since she was a child.

She had always intended to be a teacher. She believed it to be her vocation and held many strong views on education. She was clever without being brilliant, and diligent, so had done well at her tertiary studies. Her tutors had encouraged her to an honours year, her levels were good enough, but Jane's parents, anxious to see her employed and holding the value of earning a wage above anything else, eventually talked her out of it. Her major had been Australian history, and her particular interest and in a vague way her hero was Captain James Cook. It was largely her enthusiasm to write a thesis on Cook that had interested her in honours. She particularly admired virtues such as courage and fair-mindedness and was excited by the idea of adventure. She was struck by Slessor's poem on Cook:

> Cook was a captain of the sailing days
> When sea-captains were kings like this,
> Not cold executives of company-rules
> Cracking their boilers for a dividend.

At heart, Jane was a romantic idealist, though would have been surprised to hear herself described as such. Cook, alone of the great men who figured in Australian history, appeared unsullied in her mind, qualitatively different to the later settlers and explorers who she felt had, by and large, compromised themselves and their country, particularly in relation to the indigenous inhabitants.

This general prejudice against her forefathers was partly formed and largely intensified by her absorption of current popular ideologies circulating on campus. Although she had missed out on the reputedly great student movements of the late sixties and early seventies, or their adaptations in Australia anyway, she had inhaled their lingering odours which were the prevailing myths of her own time. So she was a keen conservationist, a strong land rights proponent, pro-ethnic, sympathetic to radical feminism and an ardent pacifist, which in the credo of the day also meant she was anti-American, anti-big business, distrustful of men and a disillusioned Labor voter. Physically she was unprepossessing: a small straight frame and a sharp pretty face framed by thick unruly auburn hair. Because she was slight and unassuming, she was not a girl young men had generally noticed. This did not unduly concern her, for, although heterosexual, she had not met many men she thought she liked. She had never had a lover and never strongly desired one. She felt there was plenty of time for that type of thing later, her career would take up all her energies for the present.

It was the prospect of that career, and her hopes for the future that now preoccupied her thinking. It was Friday evening. She had given herself a few days to settle in and would be starting the new term on Tuesday, which was the last term of the year. When Jane thought of what she hoped to accomplish, her heart swelled with hope and excitement. It would not be easy, she knew, thirty country kids of all ages and abilities under one roof and beholden only to her. But then she loved the idea of challenge and doing it all herself. And she was not afraid of hard work.

She would never be like the secondary teachers she had been forced to suffer under, mostly spinsters seemingly crabbed with premature age and bitterness, a narrow, constricted world compared to that of Sydney University. In all her high school days she had not one teacher she could admire. But Jane would teach with understanding and enthusiasm, instilling into her charges a genuine love of learning. She would stimulate and guide their natural curiosity, be aware of their individual talents, constructively responsive, and give to them precious things that they would carry with them all their lives, such as she had finally managed to obtain herself from her education. And in little Birra she would be far from the dry bureaucratic hand of the Department.

Jane had an instinctive dislike of bureaucracies with their petty politics and waste of funds. It was here in the field she believed that the real work was done. If she ever managed to get herself into a position of authority, what a shake-up she would give them all! She thought often of all her far-flung ideals for the betterment of secondary education in the state. It was as though they were all in many ways still in the dark ages. There was so much to be done, and so many who were incapable, even if they had some notion of what they ought to be about. And here she was, now, at the very start of it all. Who could possibly say where she would end up? She knew she would come out of this particular job a fine experienced teacher, strengthened in her resolves and with a greater ability to effect them. Beyond this, her daydreaming knew no bounds.

With these heady notions in mind, the following morning she drove out to see the school. This, surprisingly, turned out to be one hour from the centre of town. It was a hot bright Saturday, although large clouds floated aimlessly above, occasionally blocking the sun. Around her stretched the undulating green paddocks and fields of cane awaiting the chop. Mount Warning always loomed ahead beyond the ducks and twists of the dirt road. There was only one river crossing, but it was substantial, an old unfenced narrow bridge of wooden sleepers, which Jane noted was in good repair, despite apparently having been flooded many times. The water moved in a slow muddy mass not far below the bridge's height.

The schoolhouse was locked and she had neglected to bring her key, but this was no matter. Jane was delighted with it: one sturdy large granite-hewn room topped with steep wooden shingles and a chimney, much in the style of a church. Over the tall double doors was the insignia 'AD 1872', and above this an old bell. It would be deliciously cool in the heat; she had feared a squat wooden firetrap. The grounds were basically an old fenced paddock. Around these were scattered the ruins of the defunct farming settlement that had formed the original nucleus of the district. No one lived here now and surely, Jane thought, it was high time the school was shifted to the coast. She enjoyed her sandwiches and thermos of coffee under a tall stringy-bark, one of a number of shade trees left by the farmers, then drove back to town. On the way, she thought she might as well take in a few tourist attractions while she had the time and the weather held, so she skirted Birra and headed north for Byron Bay.

Byron Bay had changed considerably from Jane's spotty childhood memory of it. Jane's grandmother had lived in Brisbane, and her parents used to stop off here regularly for a few days en route to the Queensland capital, which Jane had not visited since the old lady's death, twelve years ago. The popular coastal town had changed a little for the better and a little for the worse. Back then it was still the haunt of alternative lifestylers, mostly surfies and their girlfriends, poor peaceful people living off the dole and smoking the odd weed. It was relaxed and run-down, physically spectacular with the cape and the beaches either side. Now it had moved upmarket. Either the surfies had become gentrified or a city-weary middle class had discovered it. Bright boutiques and gift shops lined the formerly unguttered main street. There was a plaza with potted palms and a fountain, and signs from the town centre clearly marked the route to the lighthouse where previously Jane and her parents had had to follow their noses along a potholed road and then struggle up a goat track.

The new sealed way was easy and direct, but this in no way detracted from the outlook, every bit as magnificent as Jane dimly recalled. It was a reasonably clear day, a little sea mist, and from the country's most easterly point she had an untrammelled view up and down the coastline, north and south of the cape. The stiff salt breeze smarted her eyes. To the south-west she could make out Birra, imagined she could see the schoolhouse further inland, but there plainly was the long brown snake of the river, and up near the haze of its source, the prominent peak of Mount Warning dominating the backdrop of mountains.

Immediately south of her was Tallow Beach. Jane could see the original track her parents and her had taken twisting up from its northern headland. Below this, the coarse red stretch of sand was bare of people. There were only a few clumps of towels and other belongings that told of the surfers bobbing in the swell a few hundred yards out to sea off the point.

The elegant whitewashed lighthouse was not actually on the end of the point. Beyond it and the road was a small saddle which rose up to a final mound of piled rocks. Jane scrambled down and when she had reached the thinnest part of the saddle, paused to look directly below at the sea some two hundred feet beneath her. Among the darker green shadows of the rocks in the shallows near the cliff she noticed one that resembled a very large fish. As she watched it, it appeared to be slowly moving. At first she thought this was just an illusion caused by the movement of the water, but as she focused her attention she saw that the shape was indeed moving and was, in fact, a shark. Although just a shadow, the broad square shape of the snout and the casual sideways sweep of the tail were unmistakable. It seemed to be gradually edging its way up the coast.

Being a Sydneysider Jane was full of shark lore, although she had never seen one in the wild. She had seen plenty up close though at the Manly Marineland, and had shrunk back with horror from them, so weird, so prehistoric and savage, always on the move, always prowling, with strange unearthly eyes that never blinked. This particular sighting here contradicted two popularly held beliefs: firstly, that a shark never swims on the surface except when attacking on the surface, and secondly, that a shark avoids rough and rocky shallows. But this old fellow obviously didn't know any of this as he lazily skirted up the jagged coastline. Then Jane realised with a shock that he must have either swum around the surfers or between them and the point.

Obviously no one had noticed. She looked back to the small dots of floating colour. The shark was well past them, uninterested.

She started climbing quickly over the rocks to keep abreast with the creature but soon found that, although it appeared that the shark was moving with majestic slowness, in fact it was travelling far more quickly than she ever could. At first it was well behind her, now it was well in front and shortly would be out of sight.

She looked out to sea past its trajectory and spied a pod of dolphins leaping out the water, a common sight off the coast. They seemed to be leading the shark by a long tow rope. It was tagging them. It was also three times their individual length which meant it was huge. Then she noticed a dolphin halfway between the pod and the shark. Perhaps it was scouting for fish but more probably it was injured or tired. This was the game. Exploding another popular notion: that when there are dolphins around, there are no sharks. The shark seemed in no hurry. Perhaps the stray was still too close to his fellows. The dolphins and their pursuer moved beyond the point and were soon lost in the glittering blue. A flock of seagulls cried above as though privy to the spectacle. Perhaps they were. Jane turned back.

Settled in the car, she considered whether she should report the sighting. There didn't seem to be much point. She browsed her tourist guide. What else was there? She could climb Mount Warning. The mountain was in its own national park, a relatively small reserve of native tropical rainforest. A looping road led about a third of the way up its base, and from there a well-graded path ran five kilometres almost to the summit with a scramble up the last pinch. The day was still fine. There were piles of dark clouds behind the mountains but these looked static. If she was quick she should be able to make it up and down before sunset.

She hurried back out onto the highway and, after a bit of poking around, found an old winding road which, she assumed, eventually joined the road between Birra and the mountain just north of the schoolhouse.

Jane sped along this for about twenty minutes, but then confusedly seemed to be heading in the wrong direction. She persisted for a while but the mountain was passing to the south. She had driven through a few small towns. Perhaps she had inadvertently taken a wrong turning. She searched back through her mind but could not think where she could have gone wrong. She came into another hamlet, Billambin, no service station, but a broken-down hotel. She parked the car, walked up onto the veranda and purposefully pulled open the heavy wooden door of the public bar.

When her eyes had adjusted to the dark, she realised that all three occupants of the room were looking at her as though she had just landed from Mars. One of them was an ancient barmaid, hennaed hair, collapsed expressionless face caked with make-up, and the eternal fag hanging from one corner of her mouth.

Jane gingerly approached her. 'Excuse me. Could you tell me if this is the right road to Mount Warning National Park?'

'No, love. You gotta go back about five miles and take a right at Girrilong. It's a bit tricky. Lots of folk miss it.'

'Ya gonna climb the mountain today?' One of the two men in the room addressed her. He was in his late thirties but prematurely aged, probably from a combination of hard drinking and hard labour in the sun. Visually, he seemed to be composed entirely from a combination of squares. His body was squat and broad shouldered, with a neckless square head surmounted by a flat ridge of short spiky hair. His skin was brown and wrinkled and he wore the traditional blue footy shorts and blue singlet, which accentuated the deep blue of his eyes.

'Yes. Why?' she answered rather impatiently.

'Yer might be leavin' it a little late, that's all.'

'I think I can make it in time.'

He shrugged laconically and returned to his middy of beer.

'Plenty of snakes, lassie,' piped up his mate. This was a typical hard-drinking specimen in his fifties, bald as a bandicoot, with a pot belly distending the middle two red Xs of his yellow and red Fourex T-shirt.

'Last time I was up there I saw stacks of snakes. Bucketed down too.' He took a long sip on his glass. 'I guess that was a while back, though.'

Jane said thank you curtly and walked back out into the blazing light. Typical of country people to be Jeremiahs, she thought. She knew they were only trying to be helpful, and they had been helpful, but for some reason they had irritated her. She got into the car, U-turned, and drove back to the correct turn-off.

The road was not in good repair. In her impatience she drove too quickly, skidding on the dirt and gravel, risking a blow-out. She came to the river that eventually flowed out at Birra. This road had no bridge but a long weir. The crossing was much higher than that on the road to the schoolhouse and the flow was smaller and weaker, but even so Jane drove through the fast-flowing stretch of six-inch-deep water with considerable trepidation. This road would obviously be impassable in any wet weather.

After this, she followed a series of eroded gullies, losing sight of Mount Warning for a while, and then it was suddenly upon her, its unusual shape looming massively above. She steered up the road and into the empty parking bay. She looked at her watch. A little after three. She reflected that it really was late to be starting the climb, but she was determined to do it anyway.

She strode out energetically on the upwardly winding path. It was Jane's first time in a subtropical rainforest and its manifold delights fulfilled her expectations. She felt she had shifted into a radically different space. Under the protective dense canopy of foliage, the air was moist and cool. She walked on a thick path of leaves through a soft green filtered light, surrounded by enormous and fantastic vegetation: giant ferns and palms, grotesque and beautiful fungi, elkhorns and staghorns and exquisite orchids growing on huge bloodwood and box trees and rose mahogany. Occasionally she sighted ancient gnarled antarctic beeches, surviving fossils from the ice age, and huge stinging plants, vines everywhere twisting out and up, tiny mosses, enormous vegetable buttresses and, perhaps the most extraordinary of all, the giant strangler fig whose aerial roots descend from the host then thicken and fuse eventually to envelope even the mightiest trees in the forest, slowly restricting the sap flow and other vital functions until the tree finally dies and rots leaving an immense cylindrical cathedral.

All around Jane, graphically, was being played out the old grim never-ending struggle (it seems there is never enough light), yet this was mitigated in her mind by the stillness and silence and beauty. How delightful, she thought, to stroll beneath this immense and varied canopy with all things around her pristine and lovely, all things in harmony. She saw no leeches or snakes. Nothing at all seemed unpleasant or threatening in this paradise. How peaceful and relaxed she felt, as though she had finally come into her own natural environment.

The way up was well graded but unrelenting. Near the top, the vegetation changed sharply to a short dry scrubby forest. The very last stretch Jane climbed with the help of a chain, but when she finally stood on the summit, and took in a few deep breaths, she felt her efforts well rewarded.

From here she could make out the entire topography. Mount Warning was an eroded plug of what once must have been an enormous volcano. Encircling her in the distance were the peaks of the caldera, spectacular crinkled forested volcanic ridges and mountains with bright blue lakes dotted amidst the green, gradually sweeping in an increasingly dramatic line up to the Lamington Plateau at the Queensland border. The whole scene was rendered sublime by the soft hazy light of late afternoon.

Forgetting herself amidst the grandeur, Jane lingered at the summit, then descended the peak light-heartedly, her spirits high from the exhilaration of the view, and quickly began the downward path. It would be easy now, she thought, the way was clear and there was no more climbing. But the path ran on and on, seemingly longer than she remembered and, almost imperceptibly, night began to descend.

Jane hurried on but now the dark swiftly overtook her like a spirit at her back, pursuing her down the mountain. The friendly and peaceful forest turned menacing. She quickened her pace, her heart now beating furiously.

She rounded a bend too quickly and tripped over a tree root she had not seen in the murk, falling heavily on her hands and face. She sat up for a moment, dazed. She was all right, she had fallen on the soft leaves. She had to get a hold of herself. She brushed the dirt off and scrummaged in her day-pack for a small torch she had been mindful enough to include. Also she pulled on a jumper, the air had become chill, and now started to follow the path carefully and deliberately with the aid of the weak beam.

The silence was oppressive, ominous, but when it was shattered suddenly, close at hand, by some creature, she had difficulty in preventing herself from crying out. The cries and rustles of the large scrub turkeys particularly began to spook her, and then after a while she imagined every root in the shadows to be a snake. And there were cries she could not identify, strange half-articulated communications sounding as if from another world, but also sounding horribly familiar, from the world of night, of the dark.

Also she could not shake off a general and growing feeling of there being a sinister presence, something peculiar to the wilderness and yet also strangely more pervasive, something she had not at all been aware of during the light of the day. This was silliness, she knew, and yet she felt herself less and less able to fight it. She tried not to think at all, not to feel, and just walk on, one step after another.

Time passed. Then all at once she was out of the forest, and in the parking bay. There was her car just as she had left it. A nightmare lifted. What on earth had come over her? As she fitted her key in the driver's door, she noticed her hand was shaking. How stupid she was, like a child. Here she was, safe and sound, of course, and the forest was safe, it had not harmed her. She looked up at the massy silhouette of trees against the starry sky. She had just tried to do too much in one day and got overwrought. She would do the walk again sometime and start out earlier.

Jane drove slowly back to Birra, unwinding as the car ambled through the warm soft night.

She arrived home in good time and was enjoying a restorative cuppa when there was a loud rap on the door. Mrs Jeffries had promised to take Jane to the club that evening and her word was her bond. Jane had completely forgotten. She called 'Come in' and the door swung open to reveal the large figure of Doreen Jeffries and slightly smaller figure of husband Jim. Mrs was wearing another floral frock, simply a smarter version of her daytime wear. Jane imagined that she had an entire wardrobe of them. Jim Jeffries, a sun-wrinkled man of medium build with a distrusting face and thinning black hair, was wearing an ill-fitting dark purple suit, and a wide pale green tie that hung outside the coat and had on it an illustration of a palm tree on an island.

'Jane, Jim. Jim, Jane,' said Mrs Jeffries.

'G'day, Miss Spencer. Pleased to meet ya.'

They all crushed into the front seat of Jim's rusted EJ and bumped off to the local RSL. This was a club appointed in the worst taste imaginable. Jane had never seen so much orange carpet in her life. Paisley ran riot like a noxious weed. The main drinking area, reasonably full at this stage, was an enormous room with an enormous bar on one side and, lining the other three sides, a glittering army of poker machines.

'What's your poison, love?' said Mrs Jeffries above the din, once they had established a territory.

'Just a little beer, thanks.'

'New, Old or Fosters?' broke in Jim.

'It doesn't really matter. Fosters, I suppose.'

'Fosters it is then.'

Jim shuffled off to the bar.

Mrs Jeffries looked around. 'Well, love, every man and his dog's here tonight.'

This was almost literally true, Jane observed, as there were two blue heelers sniffing around the feet of the crowd for dropped chips and nuts which they nipped at with bared teeth, and an old kelpie with a grey snout asleep under one of the poker machines. Some of the men eyed Jane up and down as they talked. Their own girlfriends all seemed younger than Jane and heavily made up. She noticed that the men didn't talk to them, only to one another.

Jim returned with the drinks and Doreen sailed off to the Ladies. Jim sipped his beer and glanced around nervously. He wasn't used to making conversation with single women, or anyone for that matter. His wife usually did all the talking.

Jane broke the silence. 'It's been a lovely day, hasn't it? If it's like this tomorrow, I might go for a swim in the surf.'

'Yer all right in the surf, missie, but don't go swimmin' in the river.'

'Why not?' Jane had no intention of swimming in the muddy mangrove-lined water.

'There are a few Noahs in there, mark my words.' He spoke this last phrase with emphatic seriousness although he did not look at her at all while speaking.

'Sorry?'

'Sharks, missie, sharks.' Here, probably through shyness, his voice adopted the knowing patronising tone country folk often reserve for greenhorn city slickers. Jane had come up against this a few times now and it was beginning to grate.

'They go upstream to mate. Like the mud, they say. A young boong got took two years back. Old Joe saw a cracker just last week. Ten-footer, he reckons.' He took a long sip of his schooner.

Jane watched him drink with a certain degree of fascination. She had never seen anyone drink before with such absorption and concentration. There was almost an element of beauty about it, as though it were purely an instinctive act, involuntary, part of his very being. He smacked his foam-flecked lips with satisfaction.

'Yes, actually I think I saw one from the Byron Bay lighthouse.'

'I seen 'em meself, plenty of times. Don't go swimmin' near the mouth of the river neither. That's another favourite spot.' He took another very long sip of his schooner, so long that he found much to his surprise and disappointment, he had finished the drink. He looked at the mottled inside of his glass, a little stunned. 'Well, I guess I better fill up again. You want another?'

'I think I'm right, thanks.'

'Sure?'

'All right. If you insist.' Jane was not a big drinker. She had hardly touched her glass but didn't want to appear unsociable.

Everybody was being friendly. Jim slipped off to the bar, happy to escape. Jane stood alone, slightly self-conscious, trying to drink her beer quickly.

'Jim's not boring you too much, is he, love?' Mrs Jeffries florid face re-appeared.

'Not at all. He was just telling me about the sharks in the river.'

'Ruddy menace. Should throw in some poisoned bait and kill a few of them off.'

'You wouldn't want to do that, would you?'

'Do what?' said Jim, who had re-appeared very quickly with the drinks.

Jane took one brimming glass while juggling the other. She shouldn't have agreed to a beer. She generally found it bloated her

'I was just sayin' to Jane that we should throw in some poisoned bait into the river to kill off a few of the sharks.'

'Good idea.'

'But what about the environment? The poison will kill other creatures. And should we be killing sharks anyway?'

Jim snorted. 'They're dangerous, missie. You wouldn't be worryin' too much about the envirement if one of 'em got a hold of you.'

'Waddya mean "the enviroment"?' asked Mrs Jeffries.

'Well,' replied Jane, feeling every moment more ridiculous, 'every creature has a role to play in the natural balance, even sharks in their own way play an important part and have a right to live. You can't just go around killing animals that you don't like or that are inconvenient to you.'

'Why not?' said Jim.

'Because it's wrong, morally wrong. And it's stupid. That's what's the matter with this country. People just do what they like and they never worry about the consequences. They always have. That's why we've destroyed so much of value.'

Mrs Jeffries was watching Jane with an absolutely blank face.

Jim took another long sip of his beer. 'Well, I still reckon they're dangerous bastards and ought to be killed,' he said with a slight note of aggression, but still not looking at her.

'Tell me, how are you settling in, love?' asked Mrs Jeffries, steering a more diplomatic course.

'Very well, thank you.'

'Hope that boy of mine don't cause ya too much trouble,' said Jim. Cause if he does, you just tell me and I'll learn him a thing or two.'

'I didn't know you had a son,' said Jane, amazed for some reason that they did.

'My sister's child,' said Mrs Jeffries. 'She died givin' birth. It was out in the bush and they couldn't get her to a medico. Her old man went on the grog soon after. He was really took.'

'Speakin' of grog,' said Jim under his breath.

An old little man was nudging Mr Jeffries. He was bent double with arthritis, bare-footed in a raggedy pair of khaki King-Gee boxer shorts and a greasy dark blue singlet. His right arm was roped and knotted with sinews and noticeably larger than his left, and his supplicant face puckered like an old apple, cheeks finely meshed with a lattice of delicate red veins. Either side of a bulbous nose, two watery fish-like blinking eyes started from their sockets.

'Eh, Jim.'

No reply.

'Jim, spare us a few bob, mate? Enough for a snort.'

'Here's two bucks. Now piss off.'

'You're a trouper.' The old fellow gave what appeared to be a bow to Mrs Jeffries and Jane, and shuffled off.

'Bludger,' muttered Jim. 'That's Joe I was tellin' you about, missie, as saw the shark.' Jim related how Joe was the town drunkard, suffered but not necessarily loved by all, a cane-cutter who like himself had lost his job when the industry became mechanised. The farmers still occasionally employed him to do a little manual cutting, although this was more in the way of charity.

While Jim was speaking, Mrs Jeffries began chatting to another couple, also middle-aged but younger by about a decade than the Jeffrieses. When Jim fell silent again she introduced them: Tom Bright, who ran the general store in the main street near to the Royal Hotel, and his wife Sarah, whom Jane took an instant liking to. Sarah seemed to Jane to be the epitome of a good country soul, uneducated but intelligent and warm. She had dark olive skin and black curly hair streaked with grey. Jane wondered whether she had Aboriginal blood in her. Her husband was a solidly built man with a big open face, slow, relaxed and friendly. Both of them had very broad accents, but then again everybody seemed to. They were on their way home but Sarah Bright pressed offers of future hospitality on Jane, which she resolved to follow up.

When they left, Jim Jeffries went to the bar for more drinks and Doreen recited her favourite recipes. Jane listened patiently.

Jim Jeffries returned with a young man. 'Got a fella here who's keen to meet ya, Miss Spencer. Bill Hawkins. The solicitor for the blacks,' Jim added somewhat distastefully.

'Miss Spencer. I do hope you enjoy your time in Birra.' A city accent. He shook her hand vigorously with his sweaty palm. A man in his early thirties, thin and intense with a slight stoop, body held rigid. A long thin face that might have been pleasant if not for such a pinched expression, particularly about the mouth. 'I hope you have a better time of it than your poor predecessor.'

'He deserved what he got,' replied Jim Jeffries flatly.

'Less bigotry and more understanding and he would still be here.'

'But then we would not have the pleasure of Miss Spencer,' said a deep polished voice from behind Jane.

A look of hate flashed across Bill Hawkins's face. 'I must be going,' he said. 'I'll be in touch, Miss Spencer.' He moved off.

Jane turned around. A tall, quietly imposing man was standing too close to her. Jane was now vaguely aware that he had been standing there for some time.

'Evening, Mr MacLeary.'

'Good evening, Mrs Jeffries.'

'G'day, Bob.'

'Jim, I believe this is our new teacher.'

'Jane Spencer, Robert MacLeary,' said Mrs Jeffries. 'Mr MacLeary is our local member.'

Jane shook his hand. There was a feeling of power and restraint in his grip. Physically, Robert MacLeary was an arresting figure. He was tall, well over six foot, and thin, almost gaunt, although something about him suggested great physical strength. He held himself superbly, elegant and careful in his movements, most marked in such surroundings and company. Jane also noticed he had beautiful hands. He wore a tailored suit, expensive shoes and shirt, and a loose silk cravat. She guessed his age about fifty although his skin was unwrinkled, taut in fact, his face like his body was thin and strong, but unhandsome. He had closely cropped short blond hair and pale blotches on his high forehead, which Jane guessed to be old skin cancers. The most striking feature of all were his thick sensual lips, a discordant note in a man who showed every sign of being an ascetic.

'Are you finding Birra to your liking, Miss Spencer?'

'Yes, so far. I mean, I'm sure I'll find it fine.'

'Our community needs a good teacher. It is a role of much importance, which seems to be underrated these days. Wouldn't you agree?'

'I assure you, Mr McLeary, I take my job very seriously.'

'I am pleased to hear you say it. Your predecessor was unfortunate. We are lucky to have you.'

'Perhaps you will be so good to tell me exactly what happened to my predecessor. The Department was evasive on the matter.' She was aware that with the mention again of the former teacher an embarrassment had come over the group, but Jane pressed on. She needed to know.

A slight pause and MacLeary replied, 'Certain social habits alienated him.'

'What habits?'

At Jane's question, a large loudly-dressed drunken man who had been eavesdropping the conversation spun round and thrust his sweating face at them. 'Stop stuffing around for once in your life, MacLeary, and tell the little lady what she wants to know. Sweetheart, he was screwin' the gins.'

A look of pain and anger passed over MacLeary's face. He seemed to make an effort to hold himself physically in check.

The interjector continued, 'I don't think we should be too hard on Simmons. He's hardly the first to indulge himself, didn't make a secret of it is all. The black ladies are just a little, well, easier than their white cousins.'

Jane stood speechless with indignation. She felt she was hyperventilating.

'Miss Spencer, Mr Rawson. Miss Spencer is our new teacher,' said MacLeary.

'Pleased to meet you. Matter of fact, MacLeary, while we're talking about the boongs, I've a bone to pick with you. You still set on that sewerage plant down at McMahon's Flat?'

MacLeary turned on the man, his blood clearly up. 'You couldn't possibly want that land, Rawson. It's just a bloody swamp.'

'So was Birra once.'

'In some ways, it still is. If you want to know, I'm putting the motion before council next week.'

'It's not a matter of my gain, MacLeary. It's the cost. No way you can justify it.'

'Those people should stay where they are.'

'They'll never get anywhere if they stay in that hole.'

'They'll fare even worse if they're out of it.'

'They can't be protected forever, you know.'

'I'll make a deal with you, Rawson. Hire two able-bodied blacks on your staff and I'll drop the motion.'

'You're avoiding the issue. The motion will only last as long as you're in power.'

'I have no intention of retiring from politics.'

'You may be getting a little old for it, Bob.'

MacLeary stiffened at the confidential tone. 'Mr Rawson, do you intend standing for office in the near future?'

'I've been approached. Ain't made up my mind.'

There was a pause as the two men faced off.

'Anyway,' said MacLeary in a softer tone, 'this all can't really be of much interest to Miss Spencer or Mr and Mrs Jeffries.'

Jane was peeved by his condescension, but also felt sorry for the Jeffrieses, who had been standing there dumb for the last five minutes.

A hard-faced platinum blonde in her mid-thirties came and stood beside Rawson. 'Will you be long, honey?' she whined. She was provocatively and cheaply dressed, her skin well tanned and aged before its time. She looked like a product of the Gold Coast.

'Coming now. Business.' He gave her a smile. 'Nice meeting you, Miss Spencer, Mr and Mrs Jeffries. We'll have words later, MacLeary.' He moved off with the blonde on his arm.

MacLeary watched him intensely for a moment, then turned around and deftly drew the Jeffrieses back into conversation with small-town talk.

So on her first night out in Birra 'society', Jane met the two major power brokers of the district. MacLeary had been the local member for about a decade. Descended from the original settlers of the area, last of the line, childless, a widower of an unhappy marriage, he was a private individual, not particularly gregarious, not particularly popular, but widely respected.

Rawson cut a far more aggressively public figure, and now Jane had met him she seemed to see him everywhere. A vigorous man, medium height and stocky, he boasted with truth he had never known a day's sickness, and he displayed the intolerance such people generally have towards the weak, who included all women, always falsely loud and bustling in their presence. Apparently he had been particularly scornful during MacLeary's wife's long convalescence, and even after her death.

But as Jane came to learn, his real attitude towards the 'sheilas' was more complicated. Although an inveterate chauvinist, he was highly sexed, so while he dismissed women consciously, he was affected by them, and always in their company an unacknowledged shame at this 'weakness' made him irritable and on edge, particularly after a few drinks. Far more relaxed and happy with men, he managed his urges either with prostitutes or women picked up in bars on drunken forays to the Gold Coast. It was known he particularly liked black women. He had never been able to form a stable relationship and was, more or less, by now a confirmed bachelor, but not a loner like MacLeary. He restlessly sought company as much as possible.

Jane disliked the fact Rawson was chauvinist and racist, although she found to her disappointment this was not unusual in Birra, and she bridled at his overt adoption of the ocker image, big drinking with a falsely exaggerated sense of mateship. She disliked all the braggadocio. But she hated the fact that he was corrupt. How Rawson had built his real estate fortune was thoroughly well documented by the gossips and, even if only half the stories were to be believed, his business practices were scandalous. There was little to disguise his being unpleasant, ruthless, ambitious, immoral, and yet in the way of these things, successful, powerful and well regarded.

Jane did not know MacLeary well. From a first impression he did not seem an ideal representative for the area. He was conservative, wilful and private, but no one ever said a word against his sense of probity. Rawson was clearly out to challenge him, and if he won, Jane feared for the future of the town.

Which, she soon discovered, was not the close-knit community that she had characterised all country towns as being, but basically a loosely grouped collection of homesteads and farms extending along the flat valley between Mount Warning and the sea. There was a sort of a town centre, mostly defined by the club and the pub, and this was close to the beach and the turn-off to the Pacific Highway, but some important amenities, like her school, were placed well away.

The community itself was either static, or in gradual decay. The main farming crop was sugar cane, but about a decade back sugar had begun a slow decline on world markets, three years ago it had plummeted, and presently there were no signs of any recovery. Most small farms sold out, many found themselves out of work and the larger farms, with their more efficient economy of scale, took over what was salvageable. The two biggest beneficiaries of this dislocation had been MacLeary, who now owned the single largest farm in the district, and Rawson, who owned most of the real estate. Even MacLeary had been forced to mix his farming to make it pay, and like most of the landowners now, kept sheep and cattle on his property.

The decline in prosperity caused by the sugar slump had been mitigated to some extent by a population growth of retirees immigrating north from Sydney and Newcastle. The beach-side homes had become ritzy and expensive, and again Rawson profited. The usual influx of summer tourists to the far North Coast that generally doubled the populations of Ballina and Byron Bay largely by-passed Birra, as it was away from the highway.

As far as Jane could see, there didn't really appear to be much genuine community spirit. The only time people seemed to get together was to help a neighbour with a cane burn, and these days that was less and less. There were the watering holes of course, the RSL Club and The Royal, where friendships were maintained and news and issues discussed. The town had its prominent personalities, basically MacLeary and Rawson, representing in Jane's mind the classic conflict of old and new money, and the publican of The Royal, Bill Hamblyn, who was more a figure of popular sentiment than power or wealth. There were a few local characters too, like old Joe the drunkard and Tom and Sarah Bright who ran the main store, all of whom Jane had met at the club.

There were the people of middle-ranking importance as well, and Jane as the area teacher figured herself one of these. Along with Hawkins, the white maverick solicitor for the blacks, who had now rung her a couple of times, and whom she was fobbing off until she felt more comfortable about her general situation. Other people stood out, like the owner of the local Chinese, Mr Ho and his extended family, and the Dimarcos, who ran the fruitery. But Jane never saw these people at the pub or the club, a white Anglo-Australian domain.

In fact, except for these two families, the population of the area seemed to be entirely Anglo-Celtic or Aboriginal. There was none of the diverse racial and linguistic mix that in her mind was contemporary Australia, having grown up in the nation's largest and most cosmopolitan city. Birra was like a throwback to an Australia between the wars. In terms of class and race, Jane was of the predominant group here, but notwithstanding that, she felt herself out of her element.

Throughout her life, Jane would always recall her first day at the little school at Birra, although it was upon her almost before she had time to think. Not only was it her first day as a professional teacher, but she knew from the practice teaching classes as part of her degree that the first day with any new class is of critical importance, and here more so as her class was the entire school. As far as anyone knew, Jane would be at Birra for the indefinite future, and as she drove into the schoolyard that wet Tuesday morning and parked her car in a patch of red mud, she was acutely aware that the impression she was about to make would establish her relationship with the children, and by extension possibly the entire community.

She faced the many-headed hydra of the class, fresh inquisitive faces of all variety, with considerable inward fear. But partly from her training and partly from her nature, she displayed an impressive calm and control, and after the normal tentative jousting, hesitatingly but undeniably, the class in an accord accepted her. Then the hard work began.

Jane, always a good worker, simply could not believe the enormous amount she regularly had to plough through just to keep her head above water. At first she wondered whether she was up to it, but as she knuckled down, she increasingly became convinced she was going to make a success of the job. Each week was slightly better than its predecessor, and the weeks flew past without her noticing, as every ounce of her energy and attention was absorbed.

She watched complex routines develop and become standard procedure almost of their own accord, and the children quickly emerge from anonymity as distinct individuals. Discipline and mutual respect were established without the need of excessive authoritarianism, Jane remembering with vivid anger the self-defeating hidebound arbitrary harshness of her own school days. The class slowly assumed the appearance for her of a large relatively happy family and, like any parent, she began to implement new ideas and methods with a personal force and singularity drawn from her own character and beliefs. In the standard social studies syllabus, the students were also taught about the practical and spiritual importance of conservation. In Australian history she made specific room for the woeful tale of the Aborigines under the white 'invasion', and sex education found its way into the science course, although on this last topic, Jane had considerably less experience than some of her older charges.

She felt blissfully free from the hand of a department, and this freedom carried down even to small practical matters, for example, recess (playtime) and lunch were when the children had finished what they were doing, not at eleven or one sharp. She watched over them at play like a mother hen over her chicks. The games were mostly ones from her own schooldays – Cockie Laura, French cricket, hopscotch, brandings – although these country children, on the whole, seemed more imaginative and resourceful both at work and play than she remembered her own schoolmates being. She loved the interaction of the ages too, with the youngsters gaining a few sophisticated insights and the older kids learning tolerance. Those first couple of months Jane had never been happier in her life, working hard and successfully at something she enjoyed. She had always known she was a natural teacher, and she was right.

With the children she also came to know the parents as well, and Jane gradually began to feel her way more comfortably in the community, although she was still always the 'chalkie'. Her earliest friend, after Mrs Jeffries, was the local postmaster, Mr Sims, whom she got to know in her first few weeks as she hung around the post office for mail from home. Mr Sims was garrulous but phlegmatic, with Edwardian mutton-chop whiskers and an instinctive feel and love for small bureaucracies. He was fitted to his place, benevolent despot of a happy kingdom and, like Mrs Jeffries, he was always up for a cuppa.

The son, Jonathan, seemed a carbon copy of the father, minus mutton chops, as though the mother had merely been a biological catalyst. He was a serious and steady plodder, and Jane liked him enormously both for his politeness and his commitment, as for similar reasons she quickly warmed to Hung, Mr Ho's son, perhaps also because he was a bit of an outsider like herself. So she had her favourites in the class of course, but there was no one she really didn't like. Even the 'bad' boys could generally be brought to heel. The younger ones would openly share their confidences and troubles with her, and this gave her a particular pleasure. She was popular, because she genuinely cared, and so nobody wanted to hurt her.

One pupil that particularly interested Jane was an adolescent Aboriginal girl, Jenny, who lived with her parents up at the reserve. She was about fifteen, pretty and flirtatious, and, rumour had it, promiscuous. Jane accepted this to be true after observing her with the boys in the playground. Even though she was a lively kid, she had a remarkably placid manner. She was excitable, but also relaxed and easy-going. Nothing seemed to unduly upset or disturb her. She told Jane that if she had no company, she liked nothing better than to sit still under a grove of gums at the back of her place doing absolutely nothing. This especially struck Jane, as she was a person who never did nothing.

But what drew Jane to Jenny was her latent talent. Having led a free and easy life, the girl lacked self-discipline and application, but she possessed a naturally curious and sensitive mind and Jane found that she could readily interest her in schoolwork, particularly reading, in which she would absorb herself completely if left undisturbed. When Jenny did work, she easily outstripped the other children of her age. Jane started to feed her simple novels that she had enjoyed as an adolescent, Jules Verne and *The Swiss Family Robinson*, that she was able to obtain for her from the local public library. The subsequent change in her written expression was marked, though her spoken English remained as rough as ever. After a little while, Jane began to nurture quiet, solid hopes for the girl. As she did for herself. She was so happy now she had come to Birra. She didn't mind being the chalkie. In fact, it was better in a way to have a prominent identification; it conferred a certain weight and importance. Function was a primary means of status in a country town, where even a publican, a job that hardly required outstanding abilities or intelligence, could be one of the most important figures in the community.

Which contemplation was on her mind one Friday afternoon, week over, as she sat in The Royal idly observing genial Bill Hamblyn. Jane only came to the pub occasionally. She had managed finally to develop a taste for beer, as one does in the country. Hamblyn, a jovial man with a body like an oversize fat boy, and an unruly full head of hair also like a boy's, and thick-lensed black-rimmed glasses, was not quite the full quid. It was his wife that ran the place, wiry hard-nosed Beryl, totally devoted to her husband. Bill was the front man.

At some time in the past, he had been an alcoholic, maybe it was this that had unhinged him a bit, Jane didn't know. After all, most publicans were alcoholics; it was a difficult thing for them to avoid. The odd drink with a mate over the length of the day every day invariably mounted up. They were never drunk but it hit their health just the same. Bill was now a teetotaller, he'd been on the wagon since he'd got married. Jane watched him shuffle around, collecting drinks and taking orders and chatting. Even though he was obviously simple, his opinion was sought on a range of subjects.

The talk started to irritate her, so Jane moved outside to the beer garden where she could find some peace. The men invariably preferred the cosy in-house bustle of the public bar and saloon. But while the mosquitoes out the back could be fierce, the enclosure itself was charming. Bill Hamblyn's old man had run a nursery and Bill had inherited a love of orchids. These were draped over randomly erected trellises in giddy profusion, not that they needed much nurturing in this climate. Jane briefly fingered the beautiful flowers, almost phosphorescent in the fading light, then settled down with her middy in the quiet of the dusk, relishing her solitude after a full day of clamouring, demanding, exacting charges. It was a slightly unusual sight, a single woman drinking alone, but being the teacher and an educated outsider made Jane a sort of honorary man. In the collective mind she was not grouped with the other wives and young women of Birra.

Bill Hawkins the solicitor poked his head out the back door. Maybe he wouldn't notice her.

'Mind if I join you?'

'Of course not.'

Not much of a figure for a relatively young man, she reflected as he approached. She wondered if he ate properly.

He dragged over a chair and sat down opposite. 'Hot day.'

'Very.'

'Don't often see you here.'

'I make the occasional appearance.'

'Where would Birra be without its pub? I'm sure half the citizens would go stark mad without recourse to a cold beer, myself included.' Hawkins looked directly at her with his pinched face. Even in casual conversation there was a peculiar intensity in his words.

'Have you lived in other country towns?' she asked.

'Not really. I've travelled fairly widely around the country, though.'

'How did you develop your interest in the Aborigines?'

'I grew up in Redfern. My folks are racist, naturally. Dad's a fitter, very much of his caste. As a kid and a bit later, I held their views, although we were always scared of the black kids in the playground. It wasn't until university I began to see things differently. Then I went right over. I found the people I really disliked were the silvertails I met at the uni law school. Privileged wankers. When I graduated I got myself a job with Aboriginal Legal Aid. I'm happier working for a cause. In fact, I can't see any point in working any other way.'

'I agree.'

'Thought so. I could see that the night at the RSL. Tell me, what was your impression of MacLeary?'

'Seems decent enough.'

'I guess so. I hate him, but I'm not really sure why.'

'I was much less impressed with Rawson,' she said.

'Rawson's a real bastard, no question about that. Better not talk about him, though. He's up in the public bar.'

'It was mainly what he had to say about my predecessor that got my back up.' Jane was still curious on this point.

'Simmons, yeah, he was done over properly by the town.'

'What actually happened?'

'I don't know the full story, I haven't been here that long myself. He had a girlfriend up at the reserve, one of the young girls, I don't know who it was, he was fairly discreet about it, as a matter of fact.'

'Rawson didn't give that impression.'

'Rawson, like the rest of the town, didn't know anything about it until he was actually booted out.'

'Did you know about the affair?'

'Only that there was one, and also that it was one of his pupils, nothing more. Don't think it lasted long. I'm buggered if I know how the authorities got wind of it before anyone else. I suppose you really can't have that type of thing going on. But under the circumstances, maybe a stiff word of warning would have sufficed. After all, it's hardly an unprecedented occurrence. He was sacked without notice and told in no uncertain terms to leave town. Apparently the Department of Education has completely blackballed him. The union's not interested either. MacLeary took a particularly high-toned stance on the matter, almost like he had a personal vendetta against the man or something. More political grandstanding than moral integrity, I suspect. Anyway, it's all history now.'

Jane noticed while Hawkins was talking, Rawson had wandered out. Just as well they hadn't been discussing him.

He looked drunkenly disinterested for a moment, then ambled over. 'Mind if I join ya?'

'Guess not,' said Hawkins.

Rawson pulled up a third chair. 'How are you settlin' in Miss Spencer?' His face was flushed. He stank of beer.

'Fine, thanks.'

'Top place, Birra. Best little town on the North Coast, and its going to get better. This town's got a future, let me tell you.'

'How's that?' said Jane. 'I thought the sugar industry was finished.'

'Maybe, maybe not, but that doesn't make much difference. It's land that'll push this town ahead. It's happenin' already. People like MacLeary can't ignore it any longer. It's always the same. Try to do anything and you're fightin' the bloody conservatives all the way. You'd know about that, Miss Spencer. Heard you been feedin' the kids a few new ideas.'

Play it cool, she told herself.

Hawkins gave her a quizzical look. He'd obviously been out of the town gossip.

'People with new ideas,' Rawson continued. 'Just what this place needs. Movers. People who get things done are the type of…'

He broke off as an attractive half-caste woman dressed in a smart tight pair of denims and a loose T-shirt with no bra beneath came into the beer garden through the open back gate. She brushed past the table without looking and moved quickly up towards the public bar. Rawson simply stared at her, completely ignoring everybody else. Jane felt embarrassed.

Hawkins, who had been silent since Rawson's arrival, gave a thin-lipped smile and leant forward in his chair. 'Know that woman, do you, Rawson?' he said.

'Never seen her before in my life. Who is she?'

'Dunno. Just thought by the way you looked at her you might have known her, that's all.'

'You tryin' to be funny, Hawkins?'

'Couldn't be if I knew how.'

'Yeah…excuse me.' Rawson rose unsteadily and made a beeline for the bar and presumably the girl.

He was unexpectedly frustrated in his aims by the sudden appearance in the back door of old Joe, the town drunkard who had stung Jim Jeffries at the RSL.

'Lend a mate a few bob for a beer.'

'What do you want?'

'A beer with you, mate. What about it?'

'Not now, Joe. Get out of my way.'

But it was too late. The girl had only wanted a pack of cigarettes. She re-appeared while Rawson was still wrestling with Joe and walked back across the yard and out the gate. Jane heard a car door slam, a motor start, and the sound slowly fade. Rawson stood uselessly for a moment, then swore under his breath and spat on the ground.

Old Joe hung with him. 'What about it, mate?'

'Here's five bucks, now fuck off, will you!'

'Thanks, mate.' Joe disappeared.

Rawson glanced back at Jane and Hawkins, then followed Joe back into the bar without a word.

'Rawson's in top form,' said Hawkins.

'I think he's revolting.'

'Keep an eye out for your pupils. Boredom creates opportunities for guys like Rawson. Care for another?'

'I'd better be going,' said Jane, rising.

'I'd offer you a lift but I only have a bicycle.'

'It's OK. I'm happy walking. See you later.'

'Give us a buzz if you need anything, or the town gets you down.'

'Thanks. I will.'

Jane picked up her handbag and walked out into the hot glowing dusk. Rawson with one of her pupils, what a thought! But Hawkins was right. Many of the girls were promiscuous and boredom here was a big problem. So was money, and Rawson had it. She thought of Jenny. It would probably not be long before she found herself a sugar daddy of some description.

As if in answer to Jane's thinking, one day, a couple of months into the term, Jenny came to school three hours late. Jane looked up at her sternly as she walked in, intending to leave the matter at a silent reproach, but Jenny met her glare haughtily. She sauntered up the aisle and took her normal seat in a way that attracted as much attention as possible. The class tittered.

'Come on! Get on with your work.'

They all settled down, but Jenny seemed incapable of concentrating, constantly disturbing the class in small irritating ways. Eventually, Jane had to chastise her. Because the girl knew of Jane's fondness for her, this shocked her, and she worked well the rest of the day. But for Jane, this seemed the culmination of increasingly restless behaviour displayed over the past week.

It appeared that something had happened to her and Jane was curious to find out what. During the breaks she loitered nonchalantly close to her. Jenny was not the reticent type, she was boasting, in fact, that she had found a new lover and that the find was most providential, teasing the boys, who all fancied her, quite mercilessly. It was apparently someone outside the school and presumably, if the other Aboriginal kids didn't know who it was, outside the reserve. But there was no way that Jenny could be induced to part with the identity of her lover. In fact, she seemed to display a response close to fear when pressed on this point, although Jane reasonably considered this to be an elaborate charade on the girl's part to gain maximum attention.

Whoever Jenny's lover was, he was generous. At school, Jenny invariably wore an old faded pair of jeans, a blouse, and not much else. Freedom from uniforms was another of Jane's innovations, this one more a concession to the heat and parents' poverty. Jenny began turning up in shoes and socks, shirts and dresses. Jane thought that this would invite ridicule from the other children, but she was wrong, probably because Jenny was not ostentatiously, but well dressed. And with the clothes, the girl seemed to attain a little more dignity. Her restlessness ceased, she stopped talking about her lover and even stopped flirting, and started re-applying herself to her studies.

As she succeeded with her schoolwork, Jenny began to win a grudging admiration from her classmates, and Jane's hopes for the girl once again began to rise. This affair was doing her no harm, it seemed.

Further light was cast on the business through a chance remark from Tom Bright, owner of the general store. Jane had taken a great liking to Sarah Bright at the club and, whenever she passed the store, dropped in to enjoy some friendly country gossip over the inevitable pot of tea. On this occasion, the Brights had invited her over for Sunday lunch, which meant, she presumed correctly, roast dinner.

It was a hot dry day, summer was well established now and the rains in abeyance, and Jane had left the flat without her shades, not being able to find them at the last moment. Her eyes were weak and by the time she reached the centre of town the glare was worrying her. The landscape reverberated with the heat; she could not fix it through the undulating air.

She blinked her way along the main street, almost tripping over a fat Labrador intentionally sprawled across the path, then crossed to take advantage of the long cool awning of The Royal Hotel. As she paced the flagstones she noticed approaching her at a distance the bent figure of Joe. He seemed ubiquitous. Presumably, he was seeing whether or not the pub was open, the hours being from Jane's experience somewhat erratic. She crossed back into the glare to avoid him, feeling emphatically at that moment she did not share the town's soft touch for him.

And so Jane arrived at the Brights' place with a sharp headache, which the delightful gloom of the big general store immediately relieved. Jane loved the store, which seemed to contain every manufactured item ever produced. It was more like a museum than a shop, but Tom Bright prided himself on knowing every item in stock. The Brights lived out the back in a trim cottage with a large yard where they ran chooks, and it was a hapless one of these that was lunch. This was a real home treat for Jane. She felt so comfortable with the Brights. If she ever married, she would like it to be like this; they were obviously good friends as well as good lovers. Sarah Bright largely showed her affection for her husband by teasing him, which he loved. He also loved his Sunday roast, tucking into his third helping of potatoes and gravy while his smiling wife upbraided his gluttony.

Jane chatted on about the school. The Brights had twin girls of twelve under her tutelage. They remarked that the girls had 'certainly come out with some new ideas' since Jane had begun, but did not seem displeased. Jane mentioned Jenny, how she had found herself a protector, and at that Tom's genial face darkened and he told how weeks back he had heard Rawson drunk at the club saying how much he'd like to get his end into that girl. This shocked Jane. Surely Jenny couldn't have become involved with that revolting real estate playboy. From what Jane said, Tom decided she had and the Brights agreed this was not good. They didn't like Rawson any more than Jane. And it occurred to Jane that there might be a small personal interest in this business for the Brights, as she had concluded that Sarah Bright had Aboriginal blood.

The whole native situation in Birra had begun to interest Jane, so much so that she finally decided to accept a dinner invitation with Hawkins, who had been regularly calling her and who she had been regularly fobbing off since the afternoon at the pub. They met at the local Chinese restaurant. Why she had avoided him for so long with such a string of trivial excuses she could not say.

The Green Dragon was the only 'ethnic' restaurant in the town, aside from the pizza parlour. Mr Ho's son, Hung, was one of Jane's brightest pupils. He was a child with a singular personality, often leading Jane to wonder how father and son could in any way be related. He was small, finely formed and entirely self-contained, unusual indeed for a seven-year-old boy. He invariably finished his set work before the other children, although Jane never seemed to see him working. Every time she looked up at him, he was sitting completely motionless, his hands folded on the desk, his head bowed slightly, like a little Buddha. Having finished his comprehension or multiplication, he seemed to fall naturally into a state of rapt meditation far removed from this world of vain effort and illusory hope. While his father, on the other hand, was all sweat and bustle, garrulously humble, needlessly, to his unaffected country patrons. Jane watched him now, busily juggling steaming plates around their table, his round face flattened slightly in a permanent smile. This serving ceremony had not at all disturbed Hawkins's monologue, although Jane had to admit it was an interesting monologue.

Up to now she had entertained what she believed to be reasonably well founded apprehensions concerning romantic intentions on Hawkins's part, but as he talked on and as she listened, she decided that she had been wrong here. Unless he was deeper than she thought. But no, this man showed everything on the surface, dissembling was utterly foreign to him, and he didn't seem to have a sentimental bone in his stringy body. Rather she suspected he saw her as a soulmate. As an intelligent educated radical white representing the blacks, life was bound to be lonely in a place like Birra. Tonight he seemed particularly worked up over something. Jane couldn't help noticing how much he was drinking. He had just been giving a spirited run-down of all the hopeless officials with whom he was fated to come into contact. Jane's ears particularly pricked up when he started to talk about the education coordinator for the area, Moorehead, whom she had yet to meet. Hawkins told her that his health was bad. A life of poor diet and heavy drinking had given him diabetes, and he was considering retirement.

'And do you think that will be a loss?' asked Jane, sparking off yet another outburst.

'Loss?' he cried incredulously, then checked himself and gave a small dry laugh twisting his face a little. 'You must be joking! He's just the same as the others. You've absolutely no idea, Jane. Every single bloody one of them is a corrupt, self-serving, small-minded, petty bureaucrat pissing in his mate's pocket.'

He was sounding too bitter now, an extreme bitterness usually found only in youth where it is a pose, or old age where its root is physical. But this man was neither young nor old; his bitterness derived from a genuine idealism. Jane had never met anything like it.

'I have known in this bloody place,' he continued in a softer but no less intense tone, 'only a handful of people who give a stuff about anything except their own skins and all of them, save one, maybe two, are people living in that reserve. Fine, decent, caring people who are being destroyed because they are innocent and trusting.'

'And the exceptions?'

'Me. And you, Jane.'

This introduced a personal note Jane found disquieting. He was manoeuvring her into a corner, and she didn't feel she was ready to make this type of choice, or that as yet there was any real need to. She also continued to find it odd, although a relief, that any interest that Hawkins had in her seemed as if it could only be actuated by idealism.

She had observed him carefully throughout the meal and was now completely sure on this.

'I know what you've been teaching those kids. I've heard the talk, and I've been pleased to be able to defend you. Not that everyone is critical, mind you. But it's something new for them, something different. You do know the whole town is talking about it, don't you, and I think that you are very brave. It is so essential that the kids are taught the truth if the prejudice, indifference and injustice here are ever going to begin to be addressed.'

This set Jane back a bit; she wasn't aware she was making such an impact. Now, for some reason, she decided she was not enjoying herself here and did not like this man. And she was upset at herself for not liking him. He was sincere, he was good, she agreed with all his views. Why didn't she like him? Was it because ironically, like most self-effacing idealists, those rare individuals who deny all personal needs in the greater satisfaction of becoming a general cause, he came across as conceited. He sounded full of himself because he was sure of himself. Did she, at times, sound this full of herself? He was so intense, so certain, she felt she had no room to breathe. There were no shades of grey for Hawkins, nor any for those with whom he came into contact. How limiting fanaticism was, even fanaticism that was good and right. There was something almost inhuman about it. Godlike perhaps. But since she was feeling uncomfortable, Jane thought she'd better bring the evening to a head.

'Do you remember you said that night at the RSL that you had something important to tell me? It didn't occur to me to ask you at the pub. It's something to do with the Aborigines, isn't it?'

'You should know a little of the battle between Rawson and MacLeary. They will both probably try to enlist your aid. I have a personal stake in their squabble because just at present it involves the reservation.'

'Go on.'

'Well, the history of the Aboriginal community here since the arrival of the whites has been sad and rather typical, as you may well imagine. I suppose you know that in about 1930 the New South Wales government in its sympathetic wisdom broke up all the tribes in the area and placed the people in reserves. Then to add thoughtless insult to, I admit unintended, injury, some twenty years later, a sewage treatment plant was constructed next to our reserve. Following local government ordinances, the council then set up a development ban of six hundred yards around the plant, which area largely covers the reserve. As a result, the poor people aren't allowed to build any more houses, or even upgrade the ones they're in. These are all tacky fibro affairs, never intended to be permanent, and most now are in a state of considerable collapse, which only seems to engender more antipathy amongst the white community.'

'And where do MacLeary and Rawson fit into this?'

'MacLeary wants to build a new sewage plant down on a piece of unused land called McMahon's Flat and then upgrade the reserve.'

'And Rawson wants the land.'

'Yes, but I don't know why. He says it has potential but I can't see it. I think it's just a tool in his power struggle against Macleary because, of course, MacLeary's option is the more expensive.'

'What's Rawson's option?'

'Kick the blacks off the settlement. He's parading it as an enlightened view, the time has come for these people, self-reliance, all that type of shit. He's tried to enlist my help but I refuse to have a bar of him.'

'So what's your solution?'

'I don't know. I suppose at the moment MacLeary's is the best, but he's not any more enlightened than Rawson and I think I hate him more.'

'Why?'

'Because he's a racist.'

'Come on. That's not so unusual here.'

'No, but he's a committed racist. Most people just believe what they're led to believe and so their minds can be changed, but MacLeary is different. He's thought the matter through: he wants the blacks kept in the reserve forever, believes in the supremacy of white Australia, anti-immigration, even wants segregated schools, you know, the whole bloody bit. And there's something else about him too…'

'What?'

'Dunno. Just a feeling I have. Anyway, at present the council's in a quandary and the reserve people are caught up in an inane bureaucratic bind. And while the council discusses publicly and privately various possible solutions to the impasse, old community prejudices re-surface, the boongs are good-for-nothing bludgers, they just sit around and drink, et cetera. So, for example, the unemployment problem is simply never addressed, because everyone is happy to leave the poor souls where they are and use that as a stick to beat them with. You've really no idea what the people of this town can be like…'

Hawkins continued in this vein while Jane sat silently considering the friends she had made in the community. She was also surprised to hear that there were some white men living up at the reserve. These were considered by the townspeople to be even worse than the Aborigines because, as Rawson had put it to Hawkins, 'They're only up there 'cause they can't find themselves a white sheila.' But what struck Jane most from everything Hawkins told her about the blacks was that only a handful of old men and women still spoke the language of the tribe and knew the ceremonies and myths, and they were all alcoholics.

She tried to get her head around the idea of a complete loss of language and what it might embody: the relationships to the land, the rootedness to myth and clan, the unique sense associations. She thought of everything her own language embraced, a completely discrete take on the world, a world slightly differently imagined. Surely, with the death of a language came the death of a culture. What was the answer here? What could be done? Nothing, it seemed.

'So who do you think will win this battle?' she asked finally.

'MacLeary, undoubtedly.'

'Is he really all that bad? I'm sure he's a right-wing conservative but he does seem basically decent. My landlady, Mrs Jeffries, tells me he's pretty religious.'

'Funny kind of religion that must be. I tell you I've got a feeling about MacLeary. I've got nothing on him but there's something about that man that really gets my blood up. Rawson is simple corrupt, selfish animal pleasures, girls and money and booze, but MacLeary is more subtle.'

This sounded to Jane like paranoia.

'I just don't know,' he said, shaking his head.

'What don't you know, Hawkins?' It was MacLeary's voice.

Jane and Hawkins looked up at him startled. How much had he heard?

'I don't know the solution to the reserve problem,' Hawkins replied glibly.

'He'll never have a solution,' MacLeary said to Jane. 'Dreamers never do. The blacks either stay or they go and I think you'd be better off backing me, Hawkins. If those people are let out to the mercy of the likes of Rawson, they won't survive. You know it.'

'They're not surviving very well at the moment.'

'They're doing all right. How are you, Miss Spencer? I'm sorry to interrupt your little tête-à-tête. I've had a few people to see in town so I'd thought I'd drop in here for a snack. It will be too late to rouse my cook when I get home.' He stood there casually, commandingly.

'Would you care to join us?' said Jane. It would appear rude not to offer him their company in such a small place.

Hawkins scowled and slumped back in his chair.

'Thank you.' He pulled over a chair. 'As a matter of fact, Miss Spencer, I have been meaning to speak to you. It seems that you are rewriting the history books.'

'What do you mean?' asked Jane indignantly.

'I guess it's just that I am of a different generation. I fought for my country in a war, Vietnam, completely discredited, and I come from a long line of farmers who struggled to establish themselves here. I am well off now, but I have worked hard and my family is one of many who have created wealth so that your generation can be clothed, fed and educated. Yet you teach the children that we have destroyed and wasted the land.'

'It will do these children good to know the value of the wilderness, and do them no harm to know some of the mistakes of their fathers.'

'Yet you drive a car, not a bicycle like Hawkins. You know it's easier to be idealistic if somebody else pays your wage.'

'I haven't found it very easy in this town,' said Hawkins.

'That is because you are fanatical, not merely idealistic,' continued MacLeary. 'If you wish to act upon the world, you must make some bargain with it, a compromise you would call it, Hawkins. You cannot sow and reap unless you dirty your hands.' He paused for a moment. 'But don't think I don't admire the work you both do. I do. Incidentally, Hawkins, have you considered if Rawson gets rid of the settlement he will get rid of you too? Anyway,' his voice softened, 'I dare say we all have our paths to follow. What will out, will out. Ah, here's my dinner.'

Mr Ho served MacLeary. Even though he had launched into her a bit, Jane was pleased he had turned up, saving her from the relentless Hawkins. She was tired now. MacLeary sensed this and, as he had done the night at the club, deftly steered the conversation onto lighter matters. Hawkins excluded himself, sitting back sulkily. He had no interest in or talent for trivial conversation. But Jane actually started to relax and enjoy herself. MacLeary quizzed her about the school and she was pleased to have the opportunity to talk about her small but important world.

What an odd fish MacLeary was. Sometimes he appeared to Jane like a sensitive aristocrat completely out of time and place in a parochial Australian country town, yet at other times he seemed the typical cockie, proud, snobby, arrogant, dismissing, always moving and speaking with a sense of his own importance. She had noticed at the club how he was usually surrounded by a small group of sycophants. Yet despite these disciples and the respect of the townspeople, he was personally an unpopular man, though she had never heard anyone, except Hawkins, utter a word against him. He was apparently as straight as a die, unyielding in what he saw as his moral expectations of himself and others, scrupulously fair in business matters. He was also a teetotaller, a notable rarity in such a community, and by this characteristic alone, if not by others, completely outside the mateship ethic that was so much a part of Rawson's public image. She suspected the townspeople did not like him simply because he was aloof. Jane, strangely, found this appealing.

After this evening, Jane resolved to visit the Aboriginal settlement as soon she could, which proved to be the following Sunday. It was sprinkling on and off as she took the road leading behind the town from which, after a few miles, a wide potholed dirt track lead up a denuded hill to the settlement. Jane steered her car with difficulty. A ghastly smell drifted through the cabin, the sewage plant. Imagine living next to this full time! She arrived at what she assumed must be the entrance to the reserve because of a sign, new, baldly painted in red black and yellow, declaring, 'You are now on sacred ground.' No doubt the handiwork of Hawkins.

He hadn't been able to affect much else, however, for, sacred or not, the place was a dump. There was rubbish everywhere, mostly empty bottles, but also cans, milk containers, toys and piles of old clothes. Rusted hulks of cars and scrawny dogs. Poorly dressed people, looking bored or soporific, lounging around outside shabby fibro houses.

Nobody bothered to look up as Jane drove through to the improvised centre of the buildings, parked, got out and stood awkwardly in the light rain. It was a strange slum suburb adrift. No central store or hall, no amenities whatever, no apparent infrastructure. Who had built this? Presumably the state government and the local council. And what outcome had they expected. They were simply shelving a future problem, now a present one.

She looked around, unsure what to do next. Perhaps she should visit Jenny. Close by, an overweight man in his thirties, wearing an old flanelette shirt and a threadbare pair of cords belted with rope, was sitting on a doorstep examining some nasty looking sores on his feet.

Jane approached him. 'Excuse me.'

'Yes, missie?'

She saw he was full-blood. There were not many left. His face was puffy and unhealthy, with flies crawling about his nose and eyes, but, as in the habit of country folk, he paid them no attention.

'Can you tell me where I can find Jenny Roberts?'

He left off his feet, scrutinised her, and rubbed his white chin stubble. 'She lives with her folks over there.'

'Thanks.'

The squat dwelling had not been painted in decades. At one side was a makeshift extension in wood and black heavy-duty plastic. The front door was wide open.

Jane rapped uncertainly on the lintel. 'Hello? Anyone home?'

Jenny appeared in the hallway. 'Hello, Miss Spencer.' The girl came out and sat on the front step. Her hair was uncombed. She wore a light cotton shift through which Jane could clearly see, with a shock, that she was pregnant. How many weeks? She really didn't know much about these things. 'Whatcha doing here, miss?'

'You haven't been at school for the last few days,' Jane remembered. 'I just wanted to see if anything was the matter.'

'I ain't been well, miss, that's all. I'm better now.' She grinned.

'So will I be seeing you tomorrow?'

'Sure, miss.' Jenny crouched down on the front doorstep,

Jane joined her, and they sat together a while in companionable silence.

'Here, miss, while I been sick, I made you something. Hang on.' Jenny scampered back inside the house. Shortly she returned holding two objects. 'You been so kind to me, miss. I never known no one to be so kind to me, so I made this for you, see. I got one and you got one.' She handed Jane a small clay model of a woman, crudely but artistically executed. Jenny held up her own model. The figures were identical.

Jane was touched. 'Thank you so much, Jenny. It is very kind of you.'

'This means we sisters, miss. You got one and I got one. They the only ones. We now sisters.'

Jane saw that the two models were some kind of talisman, whether traditional or individual or a combination of both it was unclear. But definitely in the girl's mind they were now bound in some significant way. 'Thank you, Jenny. I'll take care of this always.' Even Jane noticed how her voice had lost its usual schoolmistress twang.

Jenny grinned. 'We together now, miss. You will know me, miss. If something happens, you will know me.'

They sat in silence again.

'You wanna stay for dinner, miss? Mum'll be home soon.'

'Thank you, Jenny, but I have too much work to do. Another time maybe.' Jane rose stiffly. 'I'll see you tomorrow, Jenny.' She smiled at the girl and lightly took her hand.

'Righto, miss. Tomorrow.'

Jane returned past the man examining his feet. She watched him a while and he looked up and smiled good-naturedly. She smiled back and looked away. She knew nothing about these people, nothing at all. With an unidentifiable weight now on her mind, she made her way slowly to the car. Just before she opened her door, she turned to look back towards Jenny. The girl was still on the doorstep holding her model and they both waved to one another. Jane sat in the driver's seat and regarded the little gift. There was a hollow in the dashboard above the air vent to her right. She placed it in this where it fitted snugly in the moulded plastic. She would leave it there. She turned the car round and headed for home, glad she had made this visit.

As the weeks progressed and the end of the term drew nearer, Jane noticed how Jenny's relationship with the other children in the class again started to become unsettled. It was plain she was pregnant and the kids seemed to resent it, probably because it represented an unwanted and somewhat frightening intrusion of the adult world into their own.

Jenny reacted to their slow rejection by turning haughty and boastful. She told them how her child would secure her future. She would never have to live up at the reserve again and would always have nice dresses to wear. From her words, Jane wondered whether the pregnancy had been some kind of deliberate plan on her part. What was going to happen to her and the child seemed completely uncertain. No father had yet come forward and Jenny was reticent as ever, more than before, to identify him. Her increasingly strident confidence that this act would somehow better her seemed to have a desperate edge. Jane was worried for the girl.

Her behaviour in class deteriorated. She baited the other children and they bit back. One dreadful day she had a physical fight with one of the other girls, Sandra Jones, a pleasant dull-witted fatty with a fiery temper who Jenny often teased. Jane had to break them up. It was her worst day to date at the school, for the first time she had real trouble imposing discipline on the class, and at the end of it she felt utterly exhausted and depressed.

She supposed all teachers had days like this. Tomorrow, no doubt, things would be back to normal. She would place Jenny and Sandra at opposite corners of the room and keep a close eye on both. Now she really needed something to lift her spirits. The day had been fine and balmy. She decided to forget about her work and treat herself to a sunset swim in the surf.

Jane drove back to Birra, stopped briefly at home to change, then idled her car down the long Ocean Boulevard. This was prime estate. Amongst the still surviving beach shacks, most with ungainly additions funded from the rise in property values, were the signs of things to come: great sprawling glass, steel and concrete condominiums all built by Rawson in the last decade. At the very end of the street, where the bitumen ran into the sand, was his pride, Pacific Palisades, a tacky five-storey modernist monstrosity that he had somehow managed to shoehorn through council in complete contravention to regional planning restrictions. If he had his way, the whole street would be like this, en route to an eventual Gold Coast wall of high-rise.

She parked here in a little wooden corral, next to a rusty combi, grabbed her towel, and picked her way along the root-covered dirt track winding through the dense head-high scrub covering the dune backing the beach. Then she walked out to a broad glorious vista of sand, surf and rocky cliff, similar to her first sighting of Birra. She remembered that moment and the distance between then and now seemed enormous.

She was struck by the different moods this landscape could assume depending on time of day and weather. When Jane had been here last, one bright morning three weeks back, it had been bracing and windswept, the colours cold and fresh. Now all was soft and romantic, serene even. The air was still and warm and she could smell the perfume of the brush. The sky was a fuzzy dark blue gradually tending towards a shade of lilac at the horizon, the hues changing even while she watched, only about half an hour of light left. The ocean was silver-still, not even the slightest swell was visible, the only sounds the light crisping of the shore wave and the occasional far cry of a gull. The tide was out. She padded down a long hard stretch of shining sand marked with seaweed and crab burrows to the water's edge. Here, heavy clumps of rough brown kelp drifted in the shallows, not good for swimming. She decided to walk on, towards the lighthouse.

The worries of the day fell away; Jane was now completely at ease and peace. It was a paradise, a world away from the grime and fever of the big city. How could those people ever know this could be? She paused to watch tiny delicate shellfish furrow the wet sand and kicked gaily through the warm shallow breakers.

Presently she arrived at a sandy spit beyond which the river splayed through a delta into the sea. Here at this moment the world seemed subordinate to the desires of the mind, a landscape entirely empathetic. A deep thrill ran through her. She glanced around; there was no one in sight. She stripped off her one-piece and waded into the shallow water of the delta, surprised how warm it was, warmer than the sea. She ventured further; the channels deepened.

She came to a point where the colour of the water in front turned to a deep aqua. With her heart full, she pushed off into the depths. The tepid brackish medium was a delicious sensation on her body. Thick schools of angel fish swarmed around her and between her limbs. She felt herself to be part of the natural world as never before. She took a deep breath and dived beneath the surface, keeping her eyes open. The fish swam with her. She lolled on the sandy bottom ten feet below the surface, the schools wheeling around her, the surface shimmering above.

Suddenly the fish rushed away. Another similar school came rushing at her from the depths, stopped, suspended, quivering in concentration, not noticing her, then followed the others. An irrational fear struck her. Something had happened. She was out of air. She kicked to the surface and took a deep breath. How cold the air seemed! Thirty yards from her, out in the centre of the river there was turbulence. Don't be stupid, she told herself. It's simply the current of the river against the turning tide. More fish raced past. No, something had happened, was happening. Something had intruded into paradise. She measured her distance to the shore. Another thirty yards. Take it easy, take it easy, send out no distress signals. She paddled slowly. More fish raced past. She quickened her strokes. The tension and urgency seemed about to burst inside her. She looked back over her shoulder. The turbulence had gone, but there was an odd unnatural calm on the surface. She could stand it no longer. Lashing out with her legs, she sprinted freestyle to the beach. As Jane dragged herself from the water, relief overwhelmed her. She lay on her back, forgetting her nudity, panting.

Time passed. Swallows streaked overhead in the darkening sky. Jane collected her wits, dried herself, and slipped on her costume. Her hands were still shaking. She brushed back her hair and slung her towel over her shoulders. Only then did she allow herself to scan the river. Smooth as silk. Yet she had been right. Nothing could unconvince her there had been something and she had known it. And it had known her too, known her vulnerability, her fear. She shivered. Night was almost upon her. She walked back slowly in the deepening dusk.

All around was the blank empty beach, the sand a strange clammy grey. The landscape had changed again, her grand solitude now chill loneliness, with even a touch of horror in the damp air. She quickened her pace back to the car. Then, a short return of panic when she thought she wouldn't be able to locate the track taken out onto the beach, but it was clearly marked. Just nerves, she supposed. It had been a bad day.

The end of term. Jane made her farewells, packed her bags, and headed south down the highway back to Sydney and her parents' home for Christmas. As she drove, memories of the city started flooding back and she realised with a shock how completely, for a while, she had forgotten her former life. Had it only been one term? Incredible! Despite letters from home, she had managed to fully immerse herself in her new environment, or it had engulfed her. Her friends had not visited as they had promised, but then she had not even thought of them. As images of beaches and nightspots materialised, she felt herself seriously unwinding, began to see how tense, charged, she had been during the months at Birra. Well, it was to be expected, a new life with significant responsibilities. It had been great but she did need a break. Sydney in summer. Fabulous!

And the first week, at least, was blissful. It was wonderful just to rest, to have no work, no responsibilities, worries for the next day, for the next week. Then Jane began to get bored. Her time in Birra had been so full. Even with all the parties and festivities of the holiday season the city was somehow lifeless, listless. Maybe it was the heat. Her friends were still in their old ways, saying and doing the same things, even those who had found jobs. They hadn't changed at all; nothing had changed. She had changed enormously, but no one seemed to notice. Everything she did and saw and smelt and tasted took her back to what she felt she no longer was.

Yes, somehow she had left Sydney behind her; the city connected with her youth, not her adulthood. A definite line had been crossed. Now she was a professional, she had an important career. She tried to talk about this to her friends, but they seemed completely uninterested, and their conversations so trivial, about 'cute' boys and 'hip' fashions and getting 'totally wasted' at parties. Had she been like this? What did she really have in common with them?

On New Year's Eve, feigning a wooziness she actually half felt, she shied off a number of invitations and lay on her stomach on her bed reading a trashy novel. Her mind constantly drifted back to Birra, all the things she had done there, the people she had met and all of her pupils.

Particularly she thought of Jenny. The girl now avoided Jane when she tried to talk to her. Obviously the situation of her pregnancy was worrying her, and it was a worrying thing, but there seemed to be something else as well. Jane didn't know what it was, and apparently neither did the other pupils who she obliquely quizzed on the matter. Maybe Jenny herself didn't fully know what was wrong. The girl's gift was still tucked in the dashboard of Jane's car and each time she noticed it she couldn't help feeling that there had been something special between them, more so now they had drifted apart. Jenny had placed trust in her, hope perhaps that she could help her, protect her, but from what? Herself? Jane really did feel a responsibility, and a sincere affection, but if Jenny didn't give her an opening what could she do? Then again, maybe she was just being a worrier, maybe things would be all right after all. Early pregnancies in country towns were not uncommon. She was beginning to see that. And most of these matters did somehow sort themselves out in time. Still she was concerned.

After a month, Jane was bursting to get back to Birra. She left Sydney as early as she could without appearing ungrateful to her parents, who had missed her. She drove the long distance back in an almost feverish state of anticipation, although she could not have said why. When she left Sydney it was fine and clear, but typically it was raining steadily by the time she reached Birra. She was happy to be back, but somehow the wet empty streets looked foreboding. She had never liked the rain here. She climbed steps of the Jeffrieses' house and pensively opened the door of her flat. Along with the stale damp air, an unexpected surge of familiarity pushed aside all unquiet thoughts, and she realised that now she regarded this place and this town as her home.

'Jane? Love? Is that you?' Mrs Jeffries's strident tones rang out.

Jane could fairly smell the tea, and the dog. She looked around at all her books and papers, there just as she had left them, and she knew she would plunge into the new year's work with joy.

The school year began with all its usual fuss and rigmarole. Initially, Jane received the rather shocking impression that her pupils seemed to have forgotten almost everything she had taught them, but then they snapped back into routine and reluctantly but resignedly turned their energies towards their studies. A few older pupils had gone, and there were new young shiny faces to take their places, but for the most part all of her pupils were present and pleased to see her, among them little Hung, Sims junior, the Jeffrieses' boy, the Brights' twin girls, and Jenny.

Jenny was looking very pregnant. Immediately upon returning to Birra, Jane had made inquiries about her. Her situation was still unknown, still unresolved. With no father in sight, there was a growing tension in the girl's situation that went beyond the birth itself. If the father proved negligent, Jane would pursue the matter. She felt secure Hawkins would support her if things proved tricky or difficult. He might be overbearing company, but he was capable and solid as a rock. She had given him some thought while in Sydney and had softened towards him since the night at the restaurant. His work in the community wasn't easy.

Jane expected there to be friction in the class over Jenny's pregnancy, as there had been towards the end of last term, but surprisingly that proved not to be the case. Fortunately, the other children seemed to have accepted the girl's condition. Jane saw that this was because she had ceased being one of them. Once the baby was born, Jenny would not be at school any more; already she had become an adult and passed out of their world. At first they had protested, but finally they let her go with indifference. It seemed that Jane was going to lose one of her most promising pupils. She was sorry. Still, it was only a baby. No reason why Jenny couldn't be encouraged to continue with her work on a private basis; at the very least she could keep up with her reading. And she could always return to her studies later. Jane would be happy to have her at the school again, even in some kind of unorthodox arrangement. The girl was talented and Jane would not let her waste herself. She would continue to encourage and help her.

It was the wettest summer Jane had ever known. Was Birra always like this? But she had reason to think the weather unusually bad. Mrs Jeffries and Sarah Bright both commented on it, and Mr Sims, a rare complainer, grumbled to her about always having to deliver the mail in the wet, and indeed Jane noticed deliveries becoming increasingly erratic. Normally she liked the soothing patter of rain outside, but there was something unsettling in these unnaturally heavy falls punctuated by the odd wild burst. There was a sequence of cyclones up north and the Brisbane River rose and flooded part of the city. Maybe that would happen down here. Jane found it difficult to concentrate. Once home at night, she just seemed to sit at her desk with a pen in her hand and listen to the endless rattle on the roof.

So she got into the habit of working back late at the school. While the work and problems of the day were still fresh in her mind, she seemed to be able to summon up the necessary impetus to push herself. Occasionally it was dark before she left to drive home.

One Friday, a particularly bad storm appeared to be brewing. It was a sports day, but Jane had let the class go after lunch because it was simply too wet for them to be outside exercising. She worked on alone. It had been raining for weeks now in varying degrees, but independent of the consistent silver curtain, an unnatural and ominous conglomeration of heavy black clouds were presently building behind the ranges. She took a break at four for a cuppa and to catch the news on the classroom's crackly old AM radio. A severe electrical storm was descending on the area, there was a flood alert and people were warned to stay inside. A few essays to mark for tomorrow, that was all, and then she would be finished. She should make it home in time, or most of the way. She went back to it, then looked up, suddenly. Something was wrong. What was it? Silence. The rain had stopped.

She walked outside. It was prematurely dark, the air was damp and perfectly still. Enormous cumulonimbus were pushing up from behind Mount Warning. Jane had never seen clouds like these. She returned inside, switched on the light and tried to re-settle to her work. The quiet was far more disturbing than the rain. There were no birdcalls. Nothing.

As Jane applied herself to the last essay, a strange feeling crept over her. She could distinctly feel the intense gathering of the storm around. Perhaps it was the electricity, but there was a definite sense of something about to happen, even a peculiar smell in the air. Against her better sense, she became increasingly anxious. Then finally she was finished. She collected her things, locked up and raced out to the car.

But looking up at the sky she realised she had left her run too late. The storm was fairly upon her. Hopefully there would be no trouble driving back. She turned out of the yard and started along the dirt road in the deepening gloom.

Huge drops began exploding on the dusty windscreen. The sky was low and black. The storm was coming on with a swiftness that made the forecast conservative. She had been stupid. She could have easily taken the work home. Now here she was, out in the middle of nowhere, with an hour of dirt roads before Birra, and that was in fine weather. At least she had plenty of petrol.

She focused on driving quickly and safely as possible in the murky half-light. A big red 'roo bounded across the road fifty yards in front, startling her slightly. Here was an added problem. She looked around her across the overgrown fields. She could fleetingly see the small triangular heads everywhere. They must have come out thinking it was dusk, or perhaps they were animated by the precipitating violence of the weather.

A massive gust of wind caught her by surprise, forcing her onto the rough edges of the road. She steadied the car. The drops on the windscreen increased their frequency. Alternate gusts began to buffet her and lash the tops of the gums. There seemed to be movement all around. Emus were running hither and thither, comically terrified. She rounded a bend and had a brief glimpse of Mount Warning looming above her, then there was a terrific noise and all hell seemed to break loose.

The water bucketed down without respite. The noise was extraordinary. She slowed right down, switched on her lights and crawled along the edge of the road with extreme caution. The bridge must be close. How long would it take the water in the river to rise? She must keep her nerve. Sydney had its fair share of wild tropical storms but watching the spectacle from a lounge-room window was a bit different to being out on an unsealed country road in the thick of it. She remembered Sarah Bright's story of the tail end of a cyclone blowing in all the windows of their store one spring. And was the car a target for lightning? The fury increased, the noise was deafening, unrelenting. Water poured down at what seemed like an incredible volume. Visibility was virtually nil, she could dimly see the edge of the road to her left, and in front a sunburst of water, the effect of the crossed headlights moving forward into the pelting rain.

The car began to lurch into large puddles. The groundwater must be building up. She kept moving. It must ease off sometime. She crawled on for what seemed like an eternity, by her watch, twenty minutes, and was just beginning to think the situation hopeless when suddenly the fall lightened and the air cleared. She looked around. There were no animals to be seen. Rain was falling steadily on lush green fields against a backdrop of white mist. Over all was a dense ceiling of grey. Only the bottom part of the bulk of Mount Warning was visible.

Jane sped up, running a dangerous slalom around large watery potholes, hoping she would not slew off into one of the plentiful billabongs. She was anxious to reach the bridge. More twists and turns, a big dead twisted gum, she recognised the approach now, then a relatively high straight stretch, but as she accelerated along this she saw that the end of the road dipped into a mud-brown sea stretching across the entire valley, and moving from left to right with the relentless uniformity of one giant mass.

She stopped, pulled on her oilskin, and splashed out onto the road. The broad muddy sweep was colossal. Even the flood-depth poles were submerged and God only knew where the bridge was, if it still existed. At first she thought the current was slow but as she approached she realised this was an illusion from the river being so wide and straight. In reality it was fairly rushing along. Scrub, bits of wood, clumps of grass, large logs, an endless procession of huge uprooted objects swept past her, all treated with equal disdain. The rain started down more heavily. She ducked back to the car

What to do? She consulted the map. The only alternative to navigating the back roads beyond the school to Grafton and sitting it out in a hotel was an old road that swung right down to the south before heading to the coast, well below where the river should turn east to the sea. There was no knowing what condition it was in, but if she could make it through, she could then head back north along the sealed road to Birra. This route branched off about fifteen miles back. For the first twenty miles or so it seemed to travel through the MacLeary property, which presently stretched away on her right. She didn't suppose MacLeary would mind her driving through his land, particularly considering the circumstances. He wouldn't know about it anyway. She saw him in her mind's eye comfortably stretched out before a fire, sipping tea, listening to the rain providentially watering his pastures.

Jane swung the car round and headed back. Of course this other road might well be impassable, but she had plenty of fuel and daylight and was determined to try and reach the town. She found the turn-off presently. It was blocked by an old five-bar wooden gate, hammered next to it a faded sign: 'This is Private Property. No Trespassing under Any Circumstances. These grounds are Regularly Patrolled.' Silly old right-wing bastard. Jane hopped out, negotiated the gate, drove through and then carefully closed it behind her.

Amazingly, the surface seemed in reasonable repair, and despite the constant light rain, Jane started to relax and even make good time. She wound down her window to help disperse the mist that kept building up on the inside of the windscreen. If all held like this, she should be right. The road twisted south-east and soon she was running roughly parallel to the flooded river, which she could occasionally glimpse a couple of hundred yards to her left. She was fearful the road would dip down towards it, but fortunately it seemed to follow a high ridge well above the level of the swollen muddy flow.

The countryside rolled by in the rain, soft undulating bright green hills spiked with the dead stark white trunks of ringbarked gums. She imagined how this was once all rainforest. There were plenty of pockets of rainforest still extant in north-east New South Wales but they were living fossils, surviving from an earlier time when the climate was wetter, and once the forest was cut down, it did not regenerate. How she had loved being in the rainforest on Mount Warning, before the dark fell. How delightful it had been, cool and secluded, rich in life and beauty. Sydney Harbour must have once been like that, only two centuries back. What an incredible thought. What must have passed through the minds of those new settlers gazing upon the last Eden? But they were hard men, much like those up here; they could see it only as a wasteland populated by ignorant godless savages. And their dream at least had been fulfilled, beyond wildest expectations. What a leap mind and eye took in sweeping from little Cadman's cottage at The Rocks, humble in its rustic simplicity, up towards the glittering skyline at Circular Quay, hardly a stone's throw away. What a leap of worlds.

What had happened to her country? And yet the wall of hard

shining towers of wealth and work, she must be honest with herself, also contained a magnificence, although it repelled her. A masculine magnificence, a world of conflict and uncompromising self-achievement. Maybe this categorisation was sexist, limiting in its generality, yet as she drove through the lush greenery she gave herself over to these familiar prejudices. The true soul of the country, subtle and complex, balanced and harmonious, was for her a thing profoundly feminine. She thought of Jenny, and how she was a symbol of this innocent peaceful vision. A gentle spirit still moved in these hills that these settling invaders, men who had lived and worked here all their lives and who boasted they had the country in their bones, could and would never begin to understand. They were implementing an unthinking policy of slow and complete desecration.

Sydney's proud skyline, its arrogant presumption of success and power, its sense of prerogative. Something vital was there, new and strong, but something just as vital had been lost, of greater value, which had been detested, used and discarded. But could a thing so old and powerful ever be destroyed? Maybe they had just erected a veneer, a glittering facade. Maybe underneath the land still lay, patient and unyielding, unconquered, and accessible in its glory to those who could teach themselves, or bring themselves, or just let themselves feel it and open up.

BANG! She lurched forward against the belt. What the fuck! The car skidded wildly and Jane struggled to control it. She steered towards the centre of the road and braked. She had hit something. There was blood splashed on the windscreen, now streaking with the rain. She pulled on her oilskin and ran out behind the car. A wave of revulsion swept over her. She had hit a full-grown merino ram, a big one. He was quite dead, thank Christ. The head was partly smashed in, the stomach ripped open and blue steaming guts spilling out onto the road. Even in the rain, the flies were quickly gathering. It stared unblinking out at nowhere. Sheep had such funny eyes. She shivered. Nothing she could do, really.

She walked, slightly stunned, back to the car and halfway there noticed the small clay talisman that Jenny had given her lying in pieces on the road. It must somehow have been thrown out of the car from the top of the dashboard above the steering wheel through the open window. There was a muddy old scarf lying close at hand. Distressed, Jane used it to gather up the fragments. Then she happened to look up and notice the river, very close here. Down a sharp incline it rushed, only ten yards away. She watched hypnotised at the passionate violent turmoil, then looked up to her right and was surprised to see the farmhouse property about four hundred yards away. What if someone had seen her, was watching her now? There was no sign of any movement up at the house. She quickly tied her bundle and inspected the front of the car. The damage was minimal. She had hit the sheep with the centre of the 'roo bar and although this was pushed back onto the grill, the fan was free and the headlights intact. She opened the driver's door and slumped down into the seat.

What a disaster! She had begun to suspect recently that, despite all his gentry manners, MacLeary didn't like her and wanted to get rid of her. There were rumours circulating. She wasn't sure, but if they were right this would be a good opportunity. MacLeary could brand her as a lawbreaker as well as a troublemaker. No doubt he knew her area coordinator, the one Hawkins had mentioned, he seemed to know everyone of influence, and anyway with no added pressure this accident would not look good to her superiors. She was still only on trial. And then there was the expense. She had no idea what a ram like this cost but it would be in the thousands. MacLeary was certain to charge her over the trespassing and accident. There might be court costs, or at the very least a hefty fine. Perhaps he could sue her, and she had no money at all. She could deny any knowledge of it. This rankled with her conscience, and yet as she sat there in the paddock with the rain falling around, it seemed the only way out. She had never wilfully evaded responsibility. She hated to do it now; it seemed as though she was soiling herself.

She looked up at the homestead. No movement; she was sure she hadn't been seen. The dent on the 'roo bar could easily be explained, and yet…

She decided to postpone her decision until she got back to Birra. She stirred herself, started the car, and slowly drove off. The rain continued easy and the roads reasonable and she reached the town later that night without any further incident.

What a relief to be home at last after such an horrendous drive. She pulled herself out of the car and stretched out her cramped limbs, rolled her head back to release the accumulated tension. The rain still pattered lightly around. A cup of tea and then unpack the car. She grabbed her handbag and the dirty scarf with Jenny's broken talisman, both on the seat next to her.

Sitting calmly, in the lit dry flat, sipping on a cuppa, unwinding, relaxing, she realised how tired she was. Thank God tomorrow was Saturday. She placed the wet mud-stained bundle of the scarf before her and untied it. Half a dozen large pieces, but when Jane tried fitting them together she saw it was incomplete. How could she explain it to the girl? Then she noticed the scarf. It was fine silk; there was something familiar about it. Of course! It was one of MacLeary's cravats. Strange happpenstance to find it there. She finished her tea and went for the rest of her gear.

Mrs Jeffries was waiting for her in a floral nightdress and with rollers in her hair. Jane greeted her with misgiving. She didn't want to speak to anyone.

'Hello, love. Just popped out to see you were all right. Dreadful night. Heard that the river's up. Never thought you'd make it back.'

'I just got over in time.' Jane turned to hide her blush and then glanced with a sudden pang of fear towards the front of the car. Fortunately, it was hidden in shadow.

'You were lucky. Many's the time Mr Jeffries got caught out and had to stay at the Grafton Hotel. Now, is there anything I can do for you?'

'I'm fine, Mrs Jeffries. I just need a good night's sleep.'

'Best tonic in the world. I've always slept like a top meself. Mr Jeffries ain't been so lucky.'

This last comment did not surprise Jane, as at a quarter past ten on the dot every night, she clearly heard Mrs Jeffries's stentorian snores floating out into the humid night air.

'Anyway, love, goodnight to you. Sleep tight.' She waddled off into the darkness.

Jane collected her briefcase and the loose papers and books that had spilled over the back seat and the floor. With these bundled in her arms, she wearily climbed the stairs for the last time. There was pumpkin soup in the fridge, which she ate with some leftover bread. Then she went straight to bed, without even showering.

The morning was sunny. Jane rose early to get the car to the garage before anyone had a chance to comment on it. Fortunately, Mr Jeffries didn't work there Saturdays. Now she examined it more closely, she saw the damage to the front was slight. The 'roo bar had done its work. On the mechanic's advice, she decided simply to have the bar replaced. A new bar would hide most of the dents and she could have those fixed in the school holidays if she wished. She needed the car for school on Monday and could not waste time with panel beaters.

She strolled the mile or so home in the hot early morning sunshine, wishing she had remembered her hat. The air was steamy as yesterday's rains rose up from the earth. Everywhere, in gardens and vacant lots, the vegetable growth was prolific. Exotics bloomed in their natural landscape: punk-headed pandanus and the strange traveller palms, mangrove and fig sprouts, bougainvillea a riot of purple flowers over outhouse roofs and rotten backyard fences, spider ferns and passionfruit vines, banana trees and fruit-salad plants.

The Jeffrieses' front yard was an unkempt jungle, glossy green in the bright light. The plants seemed to be almost straining violently in the heat, jostling one another for the plentiful sun. She stooped down to a little jade strangled by surrounding growth. Something tugged at her mind. Her time on Mount Warning? The sun went. Large dark clouds were again pushing up from behind the ranges. She would have to get her washing out while the weather held.

Fortunately, the car was ready Monday. It had stormed intermittently over the weekend and the river was still high, though receding. One of the bridges to the north was open, so Jane could reach the school with a long detour. She had never driven this route before and it took her three hours. She arrived late, about ten o'clock. On the drive, her thoughts had dwelt on the explanation she felt she must give Jenny over the broken gift. She hated to tell her even a white lie, but Jenny was absent.

As she was the following day, which Jane gave little mind to until the unexpected appearance of the girl's mother. It was drowsy mid-afternoon, warm and overcast. Jane had set the class arithmetic exercises and most were busily bowed at these while she marked the morning compositions. There was a ripple of unrest and she followed the eyes around to a large Aboriginal woman, barefooted in a cheap cotton shift, regarding her silently from the open door of the classroom.

'You Miss Spencer?'

'Yes. Can I help you?'

'I'm Jenny's mum. You seen her 'round?'

'No. She hasn't been here yesterday or today.'

'That girl's in trouble. I know it. Trouble finds her if she don't find it. If you sees her, tell 'er her ol' man's lookin' for 'er, and he ain't happy with 'er.' With that she left. A car revved up and drove off.

Jane turned back to the class. They were chatting excitedly.

'Does anyone know where Jenny is?'

Blank looks. Silence.

'Nobody knows?'

'We ain't seen her for days, miss,' one little native girl piped up.

'All right. No more talk. Back to work.' Jane followed her own advice, but the interruption had troubled her. Jenny was caught up in something, she was sure.

That night, with the rain pattering outside, she could not put it from her mind. Maybe Hawkins might know something.

'Bill? Jane Spencer here.'

'Jane. How are you?' He could not conceal his surprise, and for the first time Jane felt comforted by that dry intense voice.

'Fine. Sorry to disturb you, but I'm worried about one of my pupils, Jenny Roberts, an Aboriginal girl. I'm sure you know her. She's pregnant and there are stories that Rawson is the father. She hasn't been in class for a couple of days and today her mother came looking for her. I don't suppose you know anything.'

'I don't know where she's run off to, if that's what you're asking me. I have been watching her situation and I'm convinced Rawson's the father. You remember what he was like that evening at the pub. I asked the girl straight out about it a few weeks back.'

'What did she say?'

'She denied she'd had anything to do with Rawson. Told me she hated him, which could well be true. But she also told me for the last year or so he had been propositioning her continually, and offering her money.'

'And you think she accepted it?'

'She wouldn't be the first girl in history to sell herself to a man that repelled her. You must have noticed the dresses she's been wearing?'

'Yes, but all that doesn't look like Rawson's style somehow. Not flashy enough.'

'She bought them herself, I guess. It doesn't take much taste to have more taste than Rawson. He's probably taken her off on a spree or something for a couple of days, not that he usually likes to be seen in the company of black women. And come to think of it, I haven't seen him around for a couple of days. She'll turn up again shortly. I wouldn't worry too much about it. These things happen. Actually, Jane, I'm glad you rang. I don't know if you've heard, but there's been some vague rumours circulating that MacLeary's out to get you.'

Jane blanched. 'I haven't heard a thing. What rumours?'

'That he's had enough of your forward-thinking ways and he's starting to make a few moves. I wouldn't be alarmed just yet. If he tries anything, I'll give you all the support I can, and you've got the good will of your pupils, and the parents too from what I gather. Also, most of this stuff I heard up at the settlement, and of course the blacks hate MacLeary.'

'Why? Other than you he seems to be the only one who's trying to help them.'

'That's true as a matter of fact, and despite my personal feelings about the man I've decided I'm definitely backing him over this sewerage plant business. But you see, as I've told you, MacLeary's a natural racist and my people know that. And they've got some funny fixation about him, worse than mine, probably because he's a figure of such power, some kind of funny superstition.'

'What kind of superstition?'

'Well, almost like he's got some strange power over people and things. I don't really blame them. He makes my flesh creep. Still, I've decided to throw my weight behind him on this particular issue. If I put my prejudices aside, I've got to admit it's better him than Rawson. Anyway, just be cautious and keep your ear to the ground. If I hear anything concrete, I'll give you a buzz.'

'Thanks.' She rang off. Was MacLeary on to her about the sheep? Hawkins said the rumours were vague. Better not to think about it. And Jenny: Hawkins seemed relatively unconcerned. She supposed he'd seen a fair bit of this type of thing. Perhaps his attitude was the right one. Still, it was worrying, and it was all a bit of a mystery.

The mystery was solved in a couple of days, but only to create a greater mystery. It was singularly the most distressing thing Jane had ever known at close quarters. Jenny turned up; part of Jenny turned up. She had drowned in the river, presumably the night of the storm, and a shark had got to her. Mrs Jeffries breathlessly described the grisly find to Jane in graphic detail. Only the upper torso had been recovered. A grim-faced mother had made the identification, the father too drunk to be of any use. No one could throw any light on the accident, and that was really all there was to it. The girl had not had a good reputation among her people, particularly latterly, and the police, generally unsympathetic in cases concerning blacks, considered they had more important matters to attend to.

The shocking death stunned Jane. She just couldn't get her head around such a terrible event. What had happened? How had she come to fall into the river? What had her last moments been like? She now realised how fond she had been of Jenny, and how much hope she had invested in her. What a waste of a life! Two lives! Now every time Jane crossed the river, still swollen from the flood, she involuntarily shivered, and there came vividly into her mind an image of the beast or beasts cruising its troubled depths.

The rain continued. The river rose again and Jane was cut off from the school. She sat in her flat, planning future lessons or reading trashy novels, continually distracted by the shifting relentless tattoo on the roof. It seemed a permanent feature. Bored, listless, she watched it from her window. Surely there could be no more water in the heavens, but down it came. Mould grew in her shoes, all shiny surfaces were wet when you touched them, the bread was only good for a day and the mosquitoes were terrible. But still it was hot, as hot as if the sun was out. It was like living in a sauna.

She had heard nothing of MacLeary's ram and was nurturing hopes the accident would be a non-event. Then one wet useless day the phone rang.

'Jane Spencer?'

'Speaking.'

'Robert MacLeary here. I wonder if I may have a few words with you about a serious matter?'

'Of course.'

'I heard you recently had an accident that damaged the front of your car, around the time of that big storm. You may or may not have heard that one of my pure-blood merino rams…'

There was a disturbance on the other end of the line. Jane heard an angry exchange. MacLeary was ticking off one of his men. She could not hear what it was about.

'Excuse me, Miss Spencer. I have to attend to something urgent. I'll call back later.'

'All right.'

The phone went dead. Jane sat down. A short reprieve. MacLeary was on to her after all. She had almost managed to put the sheep out of her mind, what with Jenny's death and everything. Now the whole dilemma faced her again. Should she lie? MacLeary couldn't possibly prove anything, or could he? If he had seen something, surely he would have come out. Perhaps she should just throw herself on the man's mercy, apologise and hope he would forget it, or come to some private arrangement which she could afford.

But admission would look bad at this stage, over a fortnight after the accident. She should have come clean at the time. But perhaps she was just saying this now she had been found out. She doubted her own motives, and still did not know how to move. She knew she would take her cue from MacLeary, put off thinking about the matter till he rang again. She felt depressed and frustrated at her impotence.

She walked downstairs to look at the car again, see if anything new might occur to her. Behind the new 'roo bar the bumper bar and bodywork was clearly pushed in and damaged. As she turned to go upstairs, something caught her eye through the window on the floor of the front passenger's seat. Jane hurriedly opened the car door and stared down at a thing that was absolutely extraordinary. There on the floor was her talisman, the one Jenny had given to her, and it was complete. She picked it up, turned it over. There was no mistaking it. So then what had she found on MacLeary's property? She raced upstairs and compared the objects. They were identical. It must have been Jenny's. What had the girl said to her? 'We sisters now. You will know me, miss. If something happens you will know me.'

Jane sat down thunderstruck and bewildered. Jenny had been

there, on MacLeary's property. Was she there the day she drowned? Jane remembered with the force of hallucination the wild muddy water so close to where she had found the doll. What had happened to Jenny on that day? There was MacLeary's scarf too.

She glanced at the phone and felt the presence of malignity allied with will. This man was evil, that was what Hawkins had originally been trying to tell her, what he did not understand himself and so now was dismissing. But he had known it just as the blacks knew. But then why did Jenny get mixed up with him? How could she have found him attractive, even loved him? Jenny was calculating, but also she was natural and passionate. She must have loved him after a fashion. Yes, and she was no innocent in these matters. The pregnancy had been contrived, but the girl had underestimated him and the whole situation. What on earth had she hoped to gain? MacLeary, she supposed. Incredible! And there was more. Jane remembered with a pang the childish delight the girl had taken in the gifts. Macleary was wealthy and powerful, but perhaps she, Jane Spencer, now had the power to break him, using Bill Hawkins as an ally. Maybe her own ghastly accident could prove providential, provide her with the means to revenge Jenny, revenge her for all the appalling indignities of her sex and race, and for the final outrage, whatever that had been. 'We sisters now.' Had she dimly foreseen it?

She looked at the squat female figure. Mere lifeless clay, yet what power it held.

Jane passed the day in torment. She felt she must come to some decision, some plan of action. She tried to think but the rain distracted her. She had listened to it so much it was now inside her head, part of her, she could not expel it.

But events moved more quickly than she could have anyway. At ten o'clock that evening, while she was clearing up after dinner, there was a harsh rap on the door. She knew it wasn't Mrs Jeffries. She had never had another visitor.

'Who is it?'

'MacLeary. Mind if I have a word with you?'

She was struck by a moment of panic. 'Just a moment.' She tried to think. Nothing occurred to her. She would have to play the whole thing by ear. As she walked towards the door she noticed the talisman and its broken replica on the table. She quickly stashed both under the couch.

MacLeary stood before her, tall, strong, with his beautiful hands and strange thick lips. He could not possibly know what had been running through her head that day. She must remember that.

'Good evening, Miss Spencer. Sorry to disturb you at this time of night but I happened to be in town. May I come in?'

'Yes, of course.'

He moved past her casually and positioned himself in the centre of the room. Jane could not take her eyes off his hands and his lips.

'A neat little place you have here.'

'Would you like a cup of something?'

'No, thank you. I saw the car downstairs, Miss Spencer. Did you kill my sheep?'

The suddenness of this caught her off guard, and she was inadvertently forced back onto her natural defences, one of which was honesty. She was not sufficiently prepared to dissemble. 'Yes I did kill it, but you know the whole thing was a terrible accident. In that heavy storm.'

'Yet you killed it while trespassing on my property.'

'It was the only way I could get through to the town. I didn't think you'd mind.'

'I mind very much. My privacy is important to me, and I particularly mind since you killed one of my prize rams. Do you have any idea how much an animal like that is worth, or for that matter what the penalties are for unlawful trespass?' His voice had become menacing. His eyes were steady, almost mesmerising.

All at once Jane sensed his capacity to concentrate thought, feeling and power, just as a lens could concentrate the life-giving sun into a beam of destruction. It was the power of the complete egoist. Hawkins too was an egoist in a way, but altruistic, self-denying, in some ways the mirror image of this man. She knew now Macleary was a secret sensualist, his passion seemingly fiercer for his ascetic mask, his close and meticulous manners. And he was seen by the townsfolk as a man of religion. Just what kind of god did he worship? She kept her eyes on him. She would not succumb. She was angry that he was humiliating and destroying her. She focused on her anger while she gathered her wits. She thought of Jenny. This was the man, and Jane had the proof.

'When I got out of my car to confirm your sheep was dead, Mr MacLeary, I found two objects on the ground nearby.'

'Some requisitioning as well as the odd slaughter?'

'I am no thief! No, you see, I thought one of them was mine, something that had fallen out of the car and broken. And the other that I gathered it in, I thought was an old rag. I realised later it was one of your scarves muddied by the rain.'

He knitted his brows slightly.

'The broken object I thought was mine, because by coincidence I had its twin mounted in the dashboard of my car. It was a small clay model of a woman made by an Aboriginal girl, Jenny Roberts, drowned in the storm, about to have a child, rumoured to be Rawson's.'

Jane had never seen such an intense look.

'How do you know the model was this girl's? It might be some standard totem the natives have been making for centuries.'

'She told me it was unique, and she wasn't lying. It was very important to her you see. She gave me its twin. The gift was a pact. She said we were sisters.'

He gave a small laugh. It made her furious. She felt the blood rush to her face.

'Think about it! Jenny told Hawkins that Rawson had propositioned her time and again, offered her money, and she found him repulsive and would have nothing to do with him. I killed your ram but it was an honest accident, even if I was dishonest afterwards. I have plenty to lose, but just maybe you have more!'

'What exactly are you saying?' His voice had assumed a tone of uneasy calm.

She wondered why she was bargaining with him, or what she was bargaining. He did think about it, though.

He put his head to one side. 'I only have more to lose if you can prove I am guilty of a crime or something. I'm not guilty of anything. I lost that scarf months ago.'

'You're lying!'

'Says who? You must admit your case is fairly flimsy, whatever it is.' He walked over to one of the lounge chairs, sat down, and crossed his long legs in an easy motion. 'Whereas as far as my merino is concerned, you have admitted to me here that you killed the animal. And in any case, a man of mine saw the accident.'

'Who? There was no one there.'

'Miss Spencer, I assure you my man Mitchell will swear in a court of law that he saw you kill that sheep. And how could you have possibly got back to Birra that afternoon without crossing my property? And what about the damage to your car?'

There was a long silence.

MacLeary reached inside his coat lapel. 'Do you mind if I smoke?'

Jane shook her head dumbly.

He took a cigarette from a flat silver box and lit it in a nonchalant fashion. 'Habit from my war years, I'm afraid. You must admit, Miss Spencer, I have you over a barrel concerning this sheep. However, that is only one of the things I wished to talk to you about tonight. There is another matter as well, probably more important.'

Jane became aware of the rain on the roof.

'Do you remember the talk we had that night in the Chinese restaurant? I've been thinking about what you were saying. It is true that I am conservative and also that I am not young. I am not prepared to stand aside for a man such as Rawson. If that is the future, God help us all. But I am prepared to bend a little, despite what people might think. Anyway, there is always room for intelligent discussion, and well-meaning people with energy.'

What was all this?

'You may have heard that the present district education coordinator is shortly to retire due to ill health. To be frank with you, I trust your discretion in these matters. The man has been ineffectual in the post, and now he is ill as well of course, and yet he lingers on. He is not interested in moving or retiring. The Department of Education and myself recognise him as a dead hand on an area that is undergoing rapid growth and change.

'The minister, partly on my recommendation, has agreed to the establishment of some two or three special positions of education coordinator, operating at a local level, but responsible directly to the department. This is basically a temporary arrangement, pending an ongoing enquiry into the long-term educational needs of the entire area. The new positions would be for people with special understanding of the local needs for modern educational development. Anyone successful in one of these jobs would have a strong claim for consideration as regional director when the present incumbent is eventually persuaded to see the light. You are a feminist, I assume you know what "affirmative action" is. The minister has informed me that special promotional opportunities for talented women are consistent with the department's new equal opportunity management plan.

'Various figures of importance here, I include myself amongst them, have been impressed with the enthusiasm and dedication that you have brought to your role as teacher for our community. I know this would be a bit of a leap of experience, and I might also add of salary, but I personally would like to see you in one of these new positions. So much so, that if you are interested then I am willing to drop my prosecution over the sheep. Any such business would obviously jettison your chances and I have been thinking that perhaps it is more important that we have capable educational coordinators, than I am compensated for the loss of a ram. I am not a poor man after all. Public duty before private concern, if you like. What do you think?'

She took her time to take it in, the lengthy silence accentuated by the rain. MacLeary smoked on, seemingly unconcerned. So, just after facing the prospect of losing her job and her possessions, she was now facing the opportunity of a lifetime. In a position like that there would be so much she could do. All her ideals.

'Anyway, Miss Spencer. Think it over. A chance like this doesn't come along very often. What is that extraordinary noise?'

'What? Oh, my landlady snoring.'

'Well?'

'Yes, all right, I'll think it over.'

'As far as my sheep goes, perhaps we could reach some arrangement. Anyway, it's late and I've taken up enough of your time.' He rose and moved towards the door. 'I'll be in touch further. Good night.' And he was gone.

She stood in the centre of the room, where he had stood. A trade-off, but one she could not possibly have anticipated. He must have been worried, she supposed. And yet he was right. What could she prove? And what would be the point of destroying herself? Jenny was dead. Nothing could bring her back. And yet there was a principle. But then again what was the point of principles if nothing could be achieved? Realistically, the only possibility of any achievement lay in the acceptance of this job. That seemed the only way she could do anything positive with her life, and yet, and yet, would Bill Hawkins have done what she was now going to do?

She bent down and brought out from under the couch the two talismans, one whole, one destroyed. Bitter tears rolled down Jane's cheeks, bitter scalding tears of self-knowledge. She held the pieces of clay tightly in her hands, until they cut into her flesh. Sisters. She did not have the strength. The rain beat down on the roof and the tears ran down Jane Spencer's sharp pretty face. The rain ran down the face of Mount Warning and into the swollen river and so on into the wide dark Pacific, that ocean of dreams from whence Captain James Cook never returned.